Paw Prints in the Ledger

by

Tara Choate

A Canine Accounting Caper

Cover Art by *Tina Lynn Stout*

The Wild Rose Press, Inc.
PO Box 708
Adams Basin, NY 14410-0708
Visit us at www.thewildrosepress.com

Publishing History
First Edition, 2025
Trade Paperback ISBN 978-1-5092-6273-1
Digital ISBN 978-1-5092-6274-8

A Canine Accounting Caper
Published in the United States of America

Dedication

To my parents.

Prologue

Irene Lisner fell in love with fraud in her eighth-grade math class.

"Who has seen Superman III?" Mr. Bearden asked the class. The group sighed at the mention of such an old movie. "You've seen it then," Bearden stated. "Does anyone remember Richard Pryor's character?"

"The computer programmer," a boy in the third row volunteered.

"Exactly. And what did he do?"

"He builds a big computer and tries to help that guy destroy the world," the boy answered, his tone indicating he was too cool to actually care. The class giggled.

"Fair enough. But I was talking about in the beginning."

No one responded. Finally, the volunteer mumbled, "I guess he stole some money."

Bearden nodded. "Technically, he used a logarithm to take a little bit of money out of a lot of people's accounts. The idea is that the embezzler created a program to round down odd cents of all the bank's accounts and deposit them into a single account. That's called the 'salami' technique. This went on for years. After enough time went by, the programmer would move the money into an interest-bearing account and start all over. In other words, he was stealing other people's money from the bank and then the bank was paying him to use it."

He looked around the room. "Does anyone know how he was caught?"

Shaking heads combined with looks of grudging interest.

"The marketing department was going through a list of names for a special promotion. The programmer had created a false name for the money and named it so it would be the last name on the customer list. Like Zyrut Zzutt. The computer logic was perfect. Then marketing decided to invite the first and last names on the customer list to a promotional event." The class giggled. "The name was so memorable that the marketing manager got curious, which ended up leading to questions."

The class giggled again.

Irene raised her hand. "You said he rounded down odd cents. Like fractions of a cent?"

Mr. Bearden nodded.

"What would have happened to them if he hadn't collected them?" Irene wondered.

Bearden grunted in approval. "The computer would have discarded them."

Irene thought about that. "So, he wasn't stealing."

"It depends on how you look at it," Bearden speculated. "No one would have come looking for the money, because accounting systems aren't set up to look for fractions of cents. But the money wasn't the computer programmer's either. Technically, it belonged to the account holders."

"But they would never have received the money," Irene protested, "so what was wrong with him finding a use for it?"

"Ah," Bearden sighed. "Now we're getting into

philosophy, which is outside the realm of logarithms." He turned to the blackboard. "If you were going to build a logarithm to lop off fractions of cents, how would you begin?"

Irene followed along with the lesson, but her mind wandered. Was the programmer stealing? If the bank was throwing the money away, what exactly was he stealing? And could such a thing be done in real life? How could you improve on the system so you wouldn't get caught?

Chapter 1

Her phone rang as she was leaving the doctor's office. "Irene Lisner," she answered smoothly.

"I need you to go to Lakelynn right now," her boss, John Fisher, barked.

"But—"

He interrupted any explanation she might have offered. "Everyone else is already out. If you weren't late, I'd probably go myself."

"I'm not late. I—"

"I know," he snapped. "I don't care. Just go."

She took a deep breath, rolled her eyes, and headed for her car. "I'm on my way. What's the story?"

"The city manager called us this morning." The "us" was the Oregon Office of Adjudication, commonly called the OA. "They discovered some missing check stock. The city manager isn't sure what to do. The city attorney suggested calling us."

"Okay," Irene opened her car door and sat down. She grabbed a legal pad and pen from the passenger sheet and started writing. "That's unusually fast. Normally they do everything they can to avoid calling us."

"We've been communicating because they're two years overdue on their audits," John admitted. "Rusty tells me they are trying to get caught up."

"The manager's name is Rusty?"

"Russell Barrett, but everyone calls him Rusty. He's

only been at the city for two months."

"Is there anything else going on I should be aware of?" Irene asked, noting down the manager's full name and time on the job.

"Yes." John blew out a breath. "Try to step carefully. The city has had negative publicity and embarrassing problems over the last few years. The previous mayor was involved in a sex scandal."

Irene raised her eyebrows. "No problem," she said dryly. "Anything else?"

"About half of the staff has left. They are doing their best to get new people hired, but it's been a challenge."

"Why? Usually, government jobs are in demand."

"The new mayor doesn't believe they should have to hire the staff to do the work. There are only a handful of people working in the entire business services section," John grumbled. "She and the council are basically at war over this situation and everything else."

Irene grunted. "Is Rusty new to the situation?"

She put her phone in the dashboard holder, swung her legs into the car, and turned on the engine. Within seconds the phone was using the car's audio system. The Oregon cloud cover made putting on sunglasses unnecessary. She backed out of the parking place to navigate toward her next assignment.

"The city council hired Rusty a few months ago and told him they wanted things cleaned up. But he hasn't made progress. He keeps saying the audits have been delayed because of the staff problems." John's tone sounded skeptical.

"But…?"

"I think they've got bigger problems."

"Such as?"

"The mayor."

Irene's brows knotted. "I'm not following. How does the mayor prevent the annual audit?"

"She thinks she's the populist politician on the rise." John's voice dripped with derision. "One of her main issues is government overspending. She wants to see the city's budget cut in half and takes any opportunity to tell the press about how they are slimming down."

"And that's keeping people away," Irene said flatly.

"It's keeping people away, but they haven't been able to get the permission to post the jobs in the first place." John sighed. "She's deadly serious about cutting the budget. But she didn't foresee that her attitude would create complications at the new high school construction."

"New high school," Irene repeated, checking her mirror as she merged onto I-5 in Salem's late morning traffic.

"I heard the rating agencies threatened to suspend the city's bond rating last week."

"Wow, that is big," Irene murmured. "So, am I going up there to sort all this out?"

She heard John's computer signal an incoming email. "Try to give me the lay of the land," he said. "The situation has been on our watch list for a while, because of the audits. But these missing checks make this a priority. I want your opinion about how bad things are."

"All right." She tapped her fingers on the steering wheel for a moment, working through her questions. In the background, she heard a rustling of paper. She moved over into the slow lane so she could set her cruise control. "Who else knows that the checks are missing?"

"I don't know. Talk to Rusty and find out what has

been going on. Try to lie low. The last thing the city needs is more media pressure."

"Of course," she said smoothly.

"Oh, and Irene?"

"Yes?"

"I've known Rusty for years, and I'd like to help him if possible."

Irene exhaled a small sigh. "Got it," she said before hanging up. She asked her phone to pull up directions for Lakelynn City Hall and sped north.

She was in the middle of dissecting the details of her doctor's appointment when her phone rang. She tapped a button. "Irene Lisner."

"Can you babysit tonight?" her younger sister, Angie, blurted. "Please. Jason wants to go dancing."

Angie had a husband, two sons, and a McMansion she could barely afford. She and Jason worked at local car dealerships. Recently, Angie had been promoted to sales manager, while Jason stayed in his sales job. Angie wanted Jason to move up to management as well. Jason didn't want the responsibility. His good looks and charm meant he had no trouble meeting his sales quota and allowed ample time for snowboarding, jet skiing, or mountain biking. The tension in the household was like a linen cloth draped over the furniture.

"Listen, Angie, I caught a new case up the valley. I'll probably have to work late and by the time I drive back, it'll be too late."

"No. It's Friday so the dealership stays open. We won't even get home until after nine."

"And the club won't get going until midnight," Irene finished for her, "so you'll want me to stay the night."

"Please."

Irene considered pretending the call dropped. She steeled herself. "Angie, I can't. I want to get to dog agility early."

Angie hung up without another word.

As this conversational ending was common, Irene spent a moment anticipating taking her dog, Percy, to the dog agility trial the next day. She and Percy were working toward a performance title and had only a few qualifying runs to go.

The phone rang again. Irene glanced at the readout before answering, thinking it was her sister calling to try again. It wasn't Angie.

"Irene Lisner," she greeted calmly.

"Hey. It's Sharon. How did the doctor go?" her friend, neighbor, and fellow dog sport competitor asked.

Irene felt her throat clog up. "It's not looking good. They said they'd have the final results next week."

Sharon made a sympathetic noise into the phone. "I think you need some time. Can you take the day off?"

"I can't. My boss called with an emergency. I'm on my way up the valley."

"Oh, for heaven's sake," Sharon growled. "You need to take it easy, not go on another case."

"Sharon, I'd rather work than sit around the house worrying about it all."

She sighed. "Right. Always under control."

Irene rolled her eyes. "I'll call you tonight."

Her friend's loud sigh came through the car's speaker. "Okay. Call me. I'm going to the library for you."

Irene smiled. "Thanks."

The phone calls had eaten up miles of road and within moments she was turning onto I-205 toward

Lakelynn. Once she took the exit, the computer took her through a major thoroughfare, a residential area, and finally an elaborate campus containing stores, including a drive-thru fancy coffee place and grocery store with government buildings tucked discreetly behind the retail establishments. Behind that, a large building was under construction. Irene judged from the extensive lawns and fields it must be the new high school. She easily found parking and studied the upscale but unremarkable modern setting. She decided to grab a coffee before checking into her assignment.

Fifteen minutes later, she walked into city hall with her favorite coffee cup filled with life-giving elixir. She took a sip and walked over the receptionist desk. "Hello. I'm here to see Rusty Barrett."

The receptionist eyed her coolly. "May I tell him your name?"

Irene eyed her back, glad she was tall enough to meet the woman's eyes in spite of the raised podium. "Irene Lisner."

Slowly, the receptionist picked up her phone and spoke quietly into the receiver. "Mr. Barrett, there's an Irene Lisner for you." With the care and precision of someone deactivating a bomb, she placed the receiver in the cradle. "He'll be out for you in a moment."

"Thank you," Irene said.

Within moments, a tall man in his forties came out from a hall to the side. He wore chinos that hung from his hips—not as though he had recently lost weight, but as though finding the right size had been more trouble than it was worth. His shoes were new, but not stylish. His button-up shirt was covered with a fleece cardigan that looked as though it would keep him warm mountaineering. The overall effect was that the assembly of this basic modern uniform required intense consideration.

He held out his hand as he strode across reception. "Ms. Lisner, thanks for coming by."

Irene rose from the chair and shook his hand. In most business settings, her simple sweater, fitted pants, and moderate heels would have been considered casual, but here it stood out as formal. She had pulled the front of her dark medium-length hair back in a barrette and wore gold hoops.

Rusty smiled warmly as Irene shook his hand. "Let's go back to my office and we can look over those papers." He gestured for her to enter the hall.

Rusty led her down a hallway and into a larger room containing several occupied cubicles. There was a small conference room forming one side and a large office along the back of the building. Rusty gestured her into the large office and offered her a chair. Even with the door shut, she felt the attention of the entire office on them through the glass. She settled into the seat.

"Thank you for coming," Rusty said earnestly. "I didn't know what to do."

"No problem," Irene said and brought out a fresh legal pad and flipped it open a new page. "Let's start from the beginning. I'm Irene Lisner and I'm with the Oregon Office of Adjudication. I work in a specialized unit of the Public Enforcement division. We work with charities and other nonprofits to enforce laws relating to their unique position of trust in the community. I understand you've been in contact with my boss, John Fisher, about the fact that Lakelynn has not filed its required annual audit. Do you have an update on the audit's status?"

"Uh, no," he stammered. "Actually, we're still waiting to get authorization."

"Okay." Irene made a note. "We'll come back to that. John told me that you are new to the City of Lakelynn. How long have you been here?"

"Yes, I was hired as city manager last month."

"Are you permanent? Interim?"

City managers were the top hired officials in any city government. They were in charge of overseeing all departments—utility, parks, finance, admin, transportation, police, fire, and any other departments the city required. Department heads reported to the city manager, who worked with them to direct information up to the city council as necessary. The city manager also acted as the chief liaison between the council and the staff, helping staff to understand what the elected officials wanted. It was a position with power, responsibility, and headaches. It wasn't uncommon for a new city manager to be hired on a trial basis.

"I was hired outright as the city manager." He reached out to take a stress ball off his desk, rhythmically squeezing it. "I thought it was a permanent job." He gave the stress ball a particularly vigorous compression. "I have no idea right now if anyone intends for that to be permanent."

"Why do you say that?" she asked.

"It's complicated." He sighed. "I don't want to waste your time when you came about the missing checks."

Irene nodded. "Is there any way to give me a short version so I can figure out if I need to come back to it?"

Again, Rusty crushed the ball before admitting, "I'm

not sure if the person who hired me had the authority to do so."

Irene made some notes. "Tell me about the checks. You're missing some check stock?" Businesses of all types purchased checks that could be loaded into a printer and used to process payments. Finance departments were careful with this check stock because of the potential dangers if some went missing.

Rusty nodded. "It looks like it, but it's hard to be sure."

Irene's eyebrows rose. "How many checks are missing?"

"We can't be sure."

Irene unclenched her jaw. "How many people know about the possible missing checks?"

"Me. The city attorney. And, of course Betty Hacher, the finance director."

Irene pressed. "No one else?"

"Not that I know of."

"All right." She paused for a moment. "All this has been discovered as a result of audit preparation, but no one has any direct knowledge or suspicion of fraud."

Rusty shook his head.

She continued. "Most people think they'll find an explanation and do everything possible to not call us. Why would your mind go immediately to fraud?"

Rusty sighed and rocked back in his chair, studying the ceiling. Finally, he said, "I'm concerned this is the tip of the iceberg."

Chapter 2

Irene studied him. "Fair enough. Let's start from the beginning."

He blew out his breath. "Okay. Well, the first thing you should probably know is that the city council hired me. When I came in for the interview, they made it clear the city was in a bit of a mess. There hadn't been a city manager for a few months. And they were very frank about the finance department needing...some work. They knew about the audits, but I'm not sure they understood the extent of the problem."

"What do you mean by that?"

"The council told me it was a delay because of turnover and some budget problems."

"And it's not?"

He rubbed his beard. "I don't think so."

"What is it, then?"

Rusty sighed again. "It started with the former mayor who was having an affair with a minor. When the whole thing came out, he made it a point to take others down with him by smearing members of the city council and the former city manager. He exposed affairs, lies on resumés, education gaps. You name it, and he made a point to let it see the light of day. Of course, the papers ate it up. Almost every one of the city councilors resigned or didn't run for reelection.

"The city manager held on for another year, marking

time, and announced his retirement before the election of the new mayor. Within a couple of weeks, the finance director had left for a new position. And within six months, approximately a quarter of the staff had left or retired.

"When the new mayor came on board, along with a completely new and inexperienced city council, there was no one to take the helm and work on finding replacements. The new mayor, Lynda Sherry, delayed hiring for every position as part of what she termed her fiscal reform platform. And the city council didn't know enough to know what they weren't seeing. It's been about eighteen months, and all the city has done is deal with emergencies.

"About six months ago, one of the city councilors came back on board. She hadn't resigned but taken a leave of absence to deal with her husband's cancer diagnosis. When she came back, she immediately saw what was going on and demanded the mayor and council find a new city manager. And so, I was hired."

"And since then?" Irene inquired, not looking up from her notetaking.

"I made it clear from the first day that my first priority was to get the finance department back on track, but it was a hard sell from the beginning. Excuses about misfiling. Misunderstandings about what was needed. Processes that weren't followed," he said, exasperation unmistakable in his voice.

"I've been trying to give the department time. You know, nudge them into shape. But frankly, I'm at my limit. Last month I made the decision to hire an auditor instead of asking them to find one. They had spent weeks claiming to be interviewing and researching companies.

When I asked for the results and they couldn't provide any, I reached out to the last auditor. No one had a problem with them, and they agreed to do it. They sent the contract, and I asked the mayor to co-sign it because the amount was over our single-signature limit."

Because her back was starting to ache and her hips were getting stiff from sitting in one position too long, Irene shifted in her chair. She took a sip of coffee and said, "Then what happened, Rusty?"

"She told me she'd get to it, then ambushed me at a full council meeting." He let out a sigh. "We record our council meetings, so it was on TV." By the look that crossed his face and the softening of his voice, she could see the memory was painful. "She got up and made a speech about government waste. She made it sound like I was presenting a contract for gold-plated toilets or something, then said she thought they were overcharging us, and we couldn't afford it. Before I knew it, the media were there, hounding me about why I couldn't increase efficiency and cut back spending."

"Mayor Sherry gave you no warning?"

He shook his head. "The next day I called the auditors. I wanted to make sure they knew we were still trying to have them come. But they told me they wouldn't put us back on the schedule without a signed contract. I called the mayor three times, trying to arrange a meeting to discuss the situation, but all I got was her voicemail."

Irene thought about it for a while. "Do you have any ideas about why the mayor is so adamant about the contract?"

Rusty shook his head wearily. "Not unless you're thinking about it in terms of elections."

Irene waited.

"The mayor wants to be governor. She's made no secret of it and tells anyone who will listen. She's been using the city as a springboard for her ideas about cutting government waste. If you know that her party was putting out a preliminary list of gubernatorial candidates at a conference this next week, you can start to see the breadcrumbs.

Irene sighed. "All right."

"The auditor wouldn't put us on the schedule, but they gave me a list of what to work on. I've been assigning out the tasks to the finance staff."

Irene nodded. "If we can get the contract signed, I'll ask them to put you back on the schedule."

Rusty grunted. "That contract will never be signed by the mayor."

"Is there another option?" she asked.

Rusty thought about it. "The council president has the authority to sign."

Irene nodded. "Will he?"

"She," Rusty corrected. "I'm sure she will. She's been the primary force pushing for us to get back on track."

"Great. Get her signature. I'll see what I can do to get you back on the schedule." Irene stood to leave.

"But wait," Rusty said. "We haven't talked about the check stock."

Irene rubbed her thumb over the tips of her fingers. "Until we get a handle on an audit, that's not going to matter."

"Auditors review statements," he pointed out. "They won't do our books."

"True. But until we have that particular stick lined

up, all the carrots in the world aren't going to make any difference." She looked at her watch. "Give me ten minutes. How long will your call take?"

Rusty shrugged. "Ten minutes should do it."

"Good. Is there somewhere I can make a call in private?"

Rusty sighed in resignation. "You can use one of the conference rooms down the hall and to your right."

"Thanks. See you in ten."

Chapter 3

Ten minutes later, Irene reentered Rusty's office. He was quickly tapping on the keyboard, clearly trying to get one more thing finished. Irene took her seat again, sipped at her now cooled coffee, and waited for him to look up. A moment later, he finished. "And send," he said, hitting a key with an extravagant motion.

"An important step," Irene said. "If you can get the contract signed by the end of the day, the auditor will have a small team begin work on Monday."

"Okay. I called Jayne. She'll be on her way in the next few minutes."

"Jayne?"

"Sorry. Jayne Tanaka, board chair. She can sign the contract."

Irene made a note. "Excellent. Now, let's talk about these missing checks."

Rusty nodded. "Like I said, I've been assigning tasks to the acting finance director, Betty Hacher. She's been working on getting the reconciliations in order."

Irene frowned. "They haven't reconciled the accounts for two years?"

"Not exactly. They've reconciled the bank statements, but didn't store the backups for the auditors to look at. When Betty went online to download and print the bank statements, she happened to notice that one of the end balances didn't match."

"How did she notice that?"

"Apparently the March statement ended with a sequence of numbers that matched her birthday. She had noticed because it was her birthday month. When she went to download the statement, the statement didn't match. She's been trying to figure out what happened ever since."

"Okay," Irene mused. "That's a first."

Rusty nodded. "When she went back to find the discrepancy, she started noticing check sequence gaps that she swears weren't there before. So, she's been spending every spare moment going back through the reconciliations, hoping to find the problem."

"Is it a batch of checks, or one or two?"

"We think it's one or two, but Monday we found more banking statements that show multiple holes in the sequence."

Irene made another note. "Okay."

"I've been working to get the auditors hired for several weeks now. I've been sending them items so they could get started on their prep work."

Irene nodded. Audits were time consuming and typically spanned several weeks or months. The first step was to amass the various information the auditors would need to begin the process: financial statements, bank statements, accounts receivable and payable reports, and other relevant documents. After these items were acquired, the audit team could begin testing the accuracy of the information. This process gave them a map for their field work.

Rusty continued, "I sent these newly found statements over to the auditors. When I called yesterday to talk to them about a contract change, they told me the statements appeared to have been modified."

"How so?"

"They showed me how the logo on these statements was different from the ones that were downloaded."

Irene blinked a few times. "The bank changed logos?"

"The statements had different logos on non-consecutive months."

Irene nodded.

"And that," he concluded, "is when I called the city attorney. And we decided to call the OA this morning."

Irene continued making notes. "Are you still struggling to find the remaining bank statements?

"Betty has found the rest of the statements, but she still can't find the originals."

"The original bank statements?"

"Yeah. They've been downloading the statements online. Right now, we have one set from the online bank and one set copied from the statements. No originals directly from the bank."

"Does the bank usually send hardcopies?"

"Yes, I called and confirmed."

Irene nodded, then flipped open her legal pad to the front page and read through her notes. A few minutes later she grunted. "Okay. Well, we've got the auditors coming. If we can get them to render a preliminary opinion, that should get us going. Talk to me about the PR situation. How many people know this whole story?"

"Well, it's all public record. As far as the missing checks go, the county's Assistant DA Gary Boyd, the city attorney, and I are the only ones who know."

"What about the issue with the bank statements?"

"Betty Hatcher and Kathy Nicols. Most of the

finance department probably thinks something is up, but I don't know how much they know. The board and mayor are aware we've been struggling with the audits, and I've told several of them about the general state of things."

"General state of things," Irene repeated. "How would you describe that?"

Rusty grunted. "Low morale. Disorganized. Not having enough or the right staff."

"Only in finance?"

"No. It's bad there, but it's hardly isolated. I can't think of a single department that's running with their entire personnel budget."

"How many departments are there in total?"

"Nine, but several of those have departments under them."

"What is your largest department?"

For a moment, Rusty looked confused but then said, "Probably the schools division."

Irene nodded. "My boss said there was some trouble with new construction?"

Rusty closed his eyes, leaned back, then studied the ceiling again. "The new high school was supposed to be a three-year build. It's been nearly five years, and they still don't have a firm move-in date. The original contract was vague, and the city has gone to court twice over disputes about materials and timelines.

"Enter Mayor Lynda Sherry," Rusty muttered darkly. "She considers the school construction enemy number one and is using it as example of everything that is wrong with governments in general. I'm not sure of the exact chain of events that caused it, but right after I started this job, the bond company called. They said they were concerned about the situation and asked to review the project. Apparently, they didn't like what they found, because they want to change the city's bond rating, which would cost us hundreds of thousands of dollars."

"What was your response?"

"I'm letting the city attorney battle it out."

Irene nodded and studied her notes. "Back to the check stock. Who has access to it right now?"

"Betty and her assistant, Kathy."

"Do you have a list of everyone who can get into the accounting program?"

"Yes. It's not a big department."

"Where are the records kept?"

"There's a records room."

"Who has the key?"

"Everyone."

"By everyone, do you mean in the department? Or in the building?"

"I mean it might be easier to make a list of who doesn't have a key."

Irene digested this bad news. "How are checks processed?"

"The staff enters the invoices and payroll, Betty makes a list, then I approve them. She cuts the checks and sends them out."

Irene took a deep breath. "Do you ever see the actual checks?"

He paused, then closed his eyes. "No. Just the list. I've been meaning to work on the process, but there hasn't been time."

Irene gazed at him impassively. "You never see or sign the actual checks or compare them to the list."

When he met her eyes, Irene thought she saw a spark

of anger flicker across his face. "I know it's not best practice."

They held each other's gaze for another moment.

"It's a common problem, especially in small departments," she admitted.

He took a deep breath, letting it out slowly. "Okay. What is the next step?"

Again, Irene shifted her weight in her chair. "We need to focus on limiting the damage while the investigation is going on."

Rusty nodded. "What should I do?"

"First, get that contract with the auditors signed. Second, find out where the checks are and confiscate them. And the signature stamp if you're using one. Stop any credit cards, including any staff purchase cards. Finally, get a locksmith in here and reissue keys only to those who need them. Don't let anyone have extra keys or keys to departments to which they are not assigned."

"That's going to cause talk."

Irene nodded. "You should prepare a staff memo indicating there have been some security concerns and that these are preemptive steps. Be direct, but don't tell anyone the whole story. You might consider a meeting with your department heads, but you should definitely set up a meeting with the city council and mayor to tell them the whole story."

"Don't you think that would alarm everyone?"

Irene studied him. "Rusty, right now, everyone should be alarmed."

"What if it the newspapers find out?"

"Work with your PR department if you have to. But you need to act sooner rather than later." She shifted gears. "Do you have an organization chart I can see?"

Rusty turned to his computer, clicked a few buttons, and quickly printed one out.

Irene studied it for a moment. "Please start setting up appointments to start interviewing the finance staff. If they—"

The door crashed open. A small dark-haired woman in her early fifties wearing a poorly cut pantsuit and way too much make-up, stood in the doorway. "Goddamn it, Rusty, now you've got the OA here. You're fired."

Chapter 4

"Couldn't you have talked to me before calling them in?" the woman sneered. "You are so fired."

Rusty took a deep breath. "Lynda, I'd like you to meet Irene Lisner. She's—"

"I know who she is," the mayor snapped. "Why is she here? Why didn't you call me?"

"Lynda, what're you hollerin' about now?"

A solid-built, white-haired man in jeans and a checked flannel shirt entered the office and gently shut the door behind him. His hair and mustache were long and completely white. The mustache was styled in a French imperial style, meaning it drooped down and then was brought up again into stiffened points. The effect was eccentric rather than trendy, though it did set him apart from other older males. Right now, his best quality was his authoritative and calming tone.

"He's got the OA here, Bill," Lynda stormed. "He's fired. We can't have this kind of publicity."

"Publicity," Bill repeated, giving Lynda a long look. When she dropped her gaze, smoothed her jacket, and sat down in one of the chairs, he turned to Irene. "I don't believe we've met. I'm Bill Henley."

She shook his hand. "Irene Lisner. I'm an investigator with the Oregon Office of Adjudication."

Bill smiled. "Well, as I'm a councilor for the City of Lakelynn, why don't you tell me about what brings you to our fine city today?"

Rusty said, "Bill, I wasn't expecting you."

Bill nodded. "Lynda called me a few minutes ago, so I thought I'd better hustle on down."

Rusty nodded. "Fair enough." He looked at Lynda. "I wasn't expecting you either."

"I should say not," she responded. "If you had, you wouldn't have called in the OA."

"Since you're here, you know there's been an incident."

Lynda looked bemused, as though she hadn't considered why Irene was there. In a much quieter voice, she said, "I didn't hear about an *incident*. I heard the OA was here."

"Okay," Rusty took a deep breath. "The other city councilors will be arriving in a few minutes. Why don't we move to a conference room?"

"Sounds like a good idea," Bill said, patting the mayor on the shoulder. The gesture appeared comforting, but Irene thought it held notes of warning and command.

"We don't need to meet," Lynda said. "We need to get the OA out of here and get rid of Rusty. Clearly, he can't be trusted."

"Lynda, calm down. No one is getting fired today," Bill said in a reasonable tone. "Let's take it one step at a time."

Irene cut in. "It sounds like it's going to be a few minutes. I'd like to take a quick break and grab a fresh cup of coffee." She returned her gaze to Rusty. "It would be nice to set up in a location that the whole office can't see."

"There's a formal conference room down the hall."

"Let's set up there. I'll be back in fifteen minutes." Without waiting for further comments or questions, Irene picked up her bag and left the office. As she walked down the hall, she heard Lynda's continuing complaints.

She glanced at the receptionist as she walked out the front door. The receptionist met her gaze with studied nonchalance, then reached for her phone.

Irene walked across the street to a small coffee shop she had spotted on her way into the city hall. As she waited to get her drink, a woman in a wide-strapped tank top and jeans came up to her side and caught her eye. "Hi."

Irene smiled back warily. "Hello."

She stuck out her hand. "I saw you over at the city hall. I'm Betty Hacher."

Irene tensed but shook her hand. "Irene Lisner."

"Are you done with your business now?" Betty inquired innocently.

Irene took her time with her answer. "I'll go back in a few minutes. I wanted a coffee."

"Yes, it's that time of day. Are you here for the day then?"

Avoiding answering, Irene picked up her drink as it was pushed across the bar. "That's my drink. Nice to meet you."

Irene slowly made her way back to city hall. The receptionist was an informant. Irene would bet it was her that had tipped off the mayor, as well as alerting Betty Hacher when she left the building. The entire office knew something was up.

Plus—Betty Hacher had something to hide.

****

Even before entering the conference room, Irene

heard Lynda's passionate voice. As though preaching at a revival, Lynda was gesturing wildly at Bill, who was seated at a large table in the center of the room. "I told you we didn't need a city manager. That's the trouble with government. All this bureaucracy just breeds more bureaucracy!" She stopped when she saw Irene.

Irene made her way to a chair, set down her bag, and brought out a legal pad. She elaborately made herself comfortable, then took a sip of her coffee.

Belatedly, Rusty got to his feet and began lowering the blinds to afford them some privacy. To fill the silence, he told the group, "We're still waiting for Jane. Robert called; he won't be able to make it."

Irene came out of her chair and moved toward the mayor. "We haven't formally met. I'm Irene Lisner from the Oregon Office of Adjudication." She extended her hand with a friendly smile.

The mayor looked taken aback for a moment, then took her hand, politician instincts taking over. "I'm sorry. I'm Mayor Lynda Sherry."

"It's nice to meet you, Your Honor," Irene said smoothly.

When Lynda offered nothing else, the room sunk back into silence. Irene returned to her chair. For the next few minutes, everyone shifted in awkward silence, trying to appear casual. Lynda tapped her fingers on the table. Bill checked his phone. Rusty shuffled papers.

An intercom buzzed. "Mr. Barrett, Councilor Tanaka is here."

"Please send her in," Rusty said, relief clear in his voice.

A pretty Japanese American woman in her late sixties entered. Her hair swept down into a stylish bob, and she had clearly come from work. She greeted the people in the room before taking a seat. Rusty immediately began making introductions again, and it was another few moments before everyone was back in their chair. He shot a nervous glance at Irene.

She stood. "I'll try to get this started. I'm Irene Lisner. I'm an investigator from the Oregon Office of Adjudication. We're all here for a purpose, so I'll get straight to the point. We've been contacted because there appear to be some accounting irregularities. The City of Lakelynn is two years behind on its state-mandated audits, which is one worrying development, but today Rusty called us after he discovered some checks are missing.

"I've been sent down here to evaluate the situation, offer some guidance, and decide what steps need to be taken. As I told Rusty, it's critical to get the auditors in here as soon as possible. I've advised him to confiscate check stock and signature stamps, and we've discussed reissuing keys to the entire staff."

When nothing came in response, she concluded. "Finally, this is the kind of thing that leads us to be concerned that some form of fraud has occurred, so I will be conducting a formal investigation. That makes it even more critical to engage an independent auditor whose audit can be conducted in conjunction with the state investigation."

Lynda came out of her chair with a roar. "You can't do that! Lakelynn is not subject to state dictates. We're in charge of our own procedure. If we want to save money by not going through unnecessary audits, then we won't do them."

Quietly, Irene said. "I'm sorry; you're misinformed.

Oregon law requires local governments to submit annual financial reports to the secretary of state."

Huffing, Lynda sat. "We'll see about that."

In the silence, Jayne Tanaka asked, "So if we agree to hire an auditor, what's the next step?"

"I've already put in a call to my team; we'll start our investigation as soon as possible. If you can get auditors in within the next few days, we'll conduct our investigation at the same time. Our goal is to assist with understanding of the law and ensuring compliance. There's a reasonable chance that all of this is a series of misunderstandings and poor judgment."

Lynda sputtered, "Poor judgment?"

"Lynda, face it." Bill said with a fair amount of weariness in his voice. "We've been fools and the world is about to know."

Rusty gave an audible sigh.

"How public will this be?" Jayne asked.

Irene thought about it. "I'm not a PR expert. From a legal standpoint, you don't have to announce anything. Unless we find something criminal, the Oregon Office of Adjudication won't need to make an announcement. But, as I told Rusty, this kind of thing is almost sure to spill out. Keeping it quiet is probably not possible. In cases like this, transparency is better than secrecy."

Bill nodded. "Make it look like we have nothing to hide."

"Then let's keep it quiet," Lynda said, jumping in. "We haven't done anything wrong. If we make a press announcement, it will look like we're admitting guilt."

"Lynda," Jayne Tanaka said firmly, "if we don't make an announcement, it'll look like a cover-up."

"I'm willing to take that chance," Lynda retorted. "I

think our staff know what they are doing. Rusty, you told me that everyone was qualified."

Rusty looked nervous. "I said that at first glance everyone seemed to have the proper training."

"See, that's what I mean?" Lynda said, looking at Rusty. "They all know what they are doing."

"But," he stressed, "I haven't had time to do any more checking."

"Why did you tell me it was all okay, then?" she snapped, belligerent again.

"It might be. It probably is," he said. "But since this is happening, I don't think that we should assume that everything is going to be fine. I think it's important to keep the facts separate from our opinions."

"No one knows how bad this could get," Jayne said quietly. All heads turned toward her. "We have a new city manager, a staff no one can vouch for, and the appearance of fiscal impropriety. The OA has arrived." She paused. "We'll make a statement."

"Jayne," Rusty said, "this is the contract with the auditors. If you sign it tonight, they've agreed to get us on the schedule as soon as possible."

As he slid the contract over to Jayne, Lynda snatched it before it reached the other side of the table. "I should be the one signing it."

"Feel free to do so," Rusty said, a note of exasperation in his voice. "But someone needs to sign it by the end of the evening, or all this is for nothing."

Lynda made a show of starting to read the contract.

"No more commentary," Jayne commanded, pulling the contract back across the table. She flipped to the last page and signed with a flourish. "Rusty, how soon will they get here?"

"They were due to come on Monday, but they told me they wouldn't come without a signed contract. They might already have someone else on their calendar."

"I spoke to the head of audit team," Irene interrupted. "With the promise of a signature, you're back on the schedule for Monday."

"Here's the contract." Jayne passed the papers to Rusty, giving Lynda a cool stare, "Make sure when you send it over that they know we're expecting them Monday."

After Rusty left the room to make arrangements to have the contract delivered, the group fell back into awkward silence. Jayne picked up the conversation. "So, what's next?"

Irene frowned. "As I said, you'll get the auditors in while I'll conduct my investigation alongside them."

Jayne shook her head. "No. What I mean is can you tell me what our next steps should be? As a council?"

Irene shook her head. "That's not my area of expertise."

"Should we call our lawyer? Have a press conference? Let things progress?"

"What do you mean press conference?" Lynda sputtered. "That's not an option."

"Everything's an option," Jayne said firmly. "I'm asking about next steps."

"The next step," Irene said gently, "is to get caught up on your audits. That's the only advice I can offer."

Jayne rubbed her forehead. "Thank you, Ms. Lisner. Let me be the first to apologize. I've had a lot going on and have been neglectful of my duties."

"Jayne, Charlie had to be your first concern," Bill murmured. "We understand."

"True, but the price of my inattention will be high."

"Well," Lynda cut in. "It wouldn't have mattered, because it's a waste of money. The only reason for an audit is to keep track of all the useless employees and give them something to do. A tight government doesn't allow for fraud."

Irene reached into her bag and drew out a brochure. "This is information about the legal and financial requirements local governments must follow to be in compliance with the state regulations. All cities, counties, and other public government entities are required to have an annual audit."

"That's ridiculous," Lynda snapped.

Irene held onto her composure. "That may be, but it is the statute."

Bill cut in. "Well, I feel like a fool. I received a letter from the state a few months ago, but didn't follow up on it."

Rusty re-entered the room and reported, "They can get here on Monday."

"Excellent," Irene said. "Let's talk more about the check stock. When is the next payroll?" She looked up. The mayor and council members looked blank.

"We pay once a month," Rusty filled in.

"That should help us avoid some hassle," she said. "A week should give the auditors enough time to know if the banking systems have been breached."

"What if they have?" Bill asked tentatively. "I mean, how many checks are we dealing with? One or two? That's all we're dealing with, right?"

Irene paused. "Mr. Henley, that's the problem. We don't know if that's all. If you weren't behind on your audits, most of this could be resolved on an internal level.

But because you are behind on your audits, the OA has to act as though the city of Lakelynn is in default. It's our duty to protect the taxpayers by making sure no money has gone missing."

"If the audits are such as big deal, how come you guys haven't done something until now?" Lynda asked, truculent to the end.

Irene gave a small sigh. "We try to go where we are wanted. If we don't get a request for help, we wait to see if the situation resolves. There is a standard timetable. I would say half of all defaults resolve without problem. But there's always someone else who wants our help."

Lynda snorted in derision. "That's a good excuse for not being more proactive."

Irene studied the woman intently. Finally, she looked down and took out her laptop. A moment later she had a recap of activity between her office and the City of Lakelynn on the screen. "First notice was nine months ago; a standard reminder that you had missed the first deadline for your annual audit. We got a response saying there had been some scheduling snafu and we'd receive the audit in a few weeks.

"Six months ago, we sent another letter. This time, Mayor Sherry wrote back and said they had decided not to do an audit. We sent letters to the entire city council, but no one responded.

"Three months ago, someone spoke to Betty Hacher. She said that you couldn't do the audit because there wasn't a city manager to oversee it. After your second annual audit was late last week, the situation was marked urgent. Someone would have been assigned to the case in the next week, but Rusty called with this situation, and that brings us up to date."

Rusty broke the silence. "I talked to Betty, and she's going to deliver the remaining check stock and signature stamps to my office later today. I've got the administrative services manager working on an email directing those who have payment cards to turn them in as soon as possible."

Irene nodded. "That sounds good. What about petty cash accounts?"

"We've been moving away from those in favor of payment cards. I've asked Betty to look up how many are in use and work on getting them returned."

"Has anyone spoken to the bank?" she asked.

"Wait." Lynda protested. "If we do all that, someone is bound to go to the press."

"That ship has sailed, Lynda," Jayne said wearily. "I don't want to do this without everyone. Someone call Robert and tell him we're going to have an emergency meeting tonight."

"I'll call him," Lynda announced. She turned to Rusty. "I know we have a public information officer on staff, but I think we should use my PR guy."

"No," Jayne and Bill answered together.

"This has to be from the city," Jayne said quietly. "It can't have a partisan slant, or even a whiff of political jockeying."

Lynda huffed. "That's ridiculous. I'm sure we could come up with something that would be fair and paint us all in a good light."

"Let's see what the publicity officer comes up with," Bill said.

"After we get the check stock and the petty cash," Rusty said, deliberately changing the subject, "where should we lock it up? Putting it in our safe might not be the right move."

"The bank should be able to help you out." Irene offered. "It would be better if no one on staff was alone with any of the items. Make it clear that a buddy system is in place. No one wants anyone to be accused of anything."

Chapter 5

Irene followed Rusty around the city offices as he gathered check stock, signature stamps, and banking documents. They had spoken with each staff person, asking them to look for any banking statements, petty cash boxes, or check stock. Rusty's tone was friendly and confiding, but a palpable waft of excitement filled the room, as though someone drenched in a strong perfume had walked through the room.

Irene was introduced as a member of the auditing team. Employees showed polite interest, wariness, and suspicion. She noticed some workers slipped out ahead of Rusty's progress through the department. Betty Hacher doggedly followed Rusty and Irene to every desk, snatching at the few pieces of paper that turned up.

After finishing the main floor, Rusty suggested a quick tour of the file room where finance records were supposed to be kept. "Maybe we can come up with a plan to unearth the rest of the records," he said hopefully. "Or even find some more check stock."

Betty looked alarmed, but followed along

They descended to the basement and Rusty used a key from a large key ring to open the door marked Finance. Irene saw file boxes stacked up and down aisles and along the walls. File cabinets hung open with folders peeking out.

"We've been understaffed," Betty said.

Rusty made a noise.

"I told you we needed more staff," she repeated.

Rusty found his voice. "Why hasn't Records been taking care of this?"

Betty looked baffled. "Records never offered."

Rusty's stunned eyes met Irene's. In sympathy, Irene said, "These things happen."

"Yeah. I don't know how many times I've told him and the mayor we need more help. They never listen to me," Betty said. "And now you're here and everyone acts like it's my fault."

Irene shifted her gaze to Rusty, who remained silent. "That's hard," she murmured.

"I mean, it's not like I'm an idiot," Betty whined. "I had my certification until I let it drop last year." She pointed an accusing finger at Rusty. "But you didn't believe me when I said we needed more help."

He closed his eyes and took a deep breath. "It's not that I didn't believe you, Betty. We've all been busy."

As though she didn't hear him, she barreled on. "I know that you're going to find a bunch of stuff. But it's the same stuff I found when I came in five years ago. You can look at my memos if you don't believe me."

Irene said firmly, "Let's not worry about how things got this way and focus on seeing if we can find anything. I assume you've gone through this area looking for banking records."

"Of course," Betty answered promptly, but her eyes skittered away. "I know how to do my job."

"Were you the only one looking for documents?" Irene queried.

"Yeah."

Irene noticed Betty's hands flexed nervously.

"Okay. Let's get the rest of the finance staff down here and see if we can put some rough order to this. We'll focus on going through things and tidying up. We can talk about doing a more thorough survey later." Irene looked at Rusty. "Does that sound fair?"

He nodded dully.

Irene shifted her gaze to Betty. "What do you think?"

Sulkily, Betty said, "I guess that's an idea."

Irene waited, but neither of her companions offered to organize the staffers.

"This isn't fair," Betty burst out. "They promoted me three years ago because they could see I knew how to do my job. I have great experience, and I'm qualified. But it's going to be all my fault because this is—" She looked around as though she could make everything return to order with the force of her stare. "—disorganized. Nobody realizes how hard I work. I mean, am I supposed to come in on the weekends to get the filing done? I used to be an auditor. I told them there was a problem, but they didn't listen to me." She threw up her hands in a motion of disgust. "I'm so insulted you're here. It's not fair."

Irene put on her best auditor's face. "Ms. Hacher, you don't have to explain to me. This process is to help the city get back on track and to ensure that the citizens of Lakelynn are protected. I hear you when you say it's been difficult, and you can be assured that everyone involved in this process will take that into account."

"What do you mean protected? Nothing is going on."

"Ms. Hacher, please understand me. I respect the difficulties you have been through. That doesn't change my job."

Her face turned red. After a moment, she said, "Fine. If you don't want to hear the story and make unfounded accusations, I can't stop you. It's always people like me who get blamed for everything." With that parting line, she stomped out the door.

Rusty sighed heavily. "I feel like such a fool. I never checked on records. If I needed anything, Betty would offer to get the item for me. I didn't think anything of it."

"Did you always get what you requested?" Irene asked quietly.

"Yes. I assumed Homer was taking care of it." Cities kept several years of financial data. Usually, two years on site and the remainder in micro fiche or some other type of long-term storage system. During an audit, determining a record-keeping procedure was a minor chore, a matter of examining the policy and then sorting through some boxes to double-check the policy was being followed.

"Homer?" Irene pressed.

"Homer Courtney. The city recorder."

"Does he file for the finance department?"

"I thought so," Rusty said weakly. "I know that Betty and he are friendly. I've certainly never heard her complain about them. And she's not shy about complaining."

Irene nodded. "Is Mr. Courtney here today?"

"He never leaves. He's never been sick, never taken a vacation day." He smiled wryly. "He might live here for all I know."

Irene thought for a moment. "Would you mind splitting up? You could get started here, and I could go talk to Mr. Courtney."

Rusty agreed. Irene moved toward a door marked City Recorder.

This office was as clean, tidy, and remarkably light. There was a counter with several workstations, some marked with specific tasks, others clearly for miscellaneous inquiries. Irene moved to the one that said *Homer Courtney, City Recorder*.

Homer Courtney was an older man with a lithe and springy build. He had a trim mustache and long hair, giving him the overall appearance of an aging tree hugger. Irene was unsurprised to see he was wearing Birkenstocks.

"Hello, Mr. Courtney. I'm Irene Lisner." She held out her hand. "I work for the Oregon Office of Adjudication. Have you heard about our visit today?"

He nodded, his eyes twinkling in indication that he had already heard all the gossip. "Nice to meet you, Ms. Lisner."

"Call me Irene."

"Sure. Call me Homer."

"Thank you. I wanted to talk to you about the finance records. Does your department take care of them?"

An angry look crossed his face but smoothed out quickly. "Not for about ten years."

"Why not?"

"The former finance director and I had an argument about retention requirements, so he always had his people do it."

Irene took out her legal pad and pen. "I take it you and he didn't get along."

"He was—" He broke off, clearly considering his words. "He was not my favorite person."

41

"Why didn't you take it back over when he left?"

"I didn't think about it, and Betty never asked," he said simply, then sighed. "I should have followed up. Betty's a good accountant, but management isn't her strong suit. She's great with the details but lets the big things get away from her. She probably kept putting things in the to-be-filed area and never checked on what was happening."

Irene nodded and looked around the offices. "I was told you didn't have any other staff."

Homer smiled. "True. But that doesn't mean I'm the only one who works down here." He nodded at a nearby desk. "That's for property taxes, but we won't see them for a few months. They work for the county." He gestured to another area. "That's for public works and utilities, but they only work part time."

Irene nodded. "Do you think you could tackle that finance room?"

He grinned. "I'd love to."

Chapter 6

Irene left the basement, intending to find Rusty. She didn't have to look far. She found him in the staff area, having a loud argument with Mayor Sherry in front of an audience of fascinated listeners.

"It's not my fault *The Herald* called," he said.

"But it's your fault the OA is here," she retorted.

Irene had been in many uncomfortable situations, often as an unofficial referee. This situation seemed particularly explosive. She considered simply leaving. When she returned on Monday with her staff, the Lakelynn leaders would either have come up with a plan or killed each other.

She approached the combatants. "I'm sorry to interrupt, but maybe we should take this into a private office?"

Both turned to glare at her. Rusty collected himself first. "Good idea."

He gestured down the hall, ultimately returning to the conference room where they had met with the city councilors earlier. Jayne Tanaka and Bill Henley were still there.

"Maybe we should contact a PR firm," Jayne said, continuing her conversation with Bill.

Lynda sputtered. "We never talked about talking to PR."

"Lynda, I think a press release is a good idea."

Looking furious, Lynda rounded on Rusty again. "You told the council about *The Herald*?"

He turned and stalked out of the room.

Jayne watched him go, clearly unhappy. "A short press release providing the facts will be a preemptive measure. We explain we're working with the state to fulfil our reporting requirements and have engaged an auditor to perform some routine oversight. We won't go into the details."

"Should we send a memo to the city staff?" Bill wondered.

Thoughtfully, Jayne nodded. "A brief memo to all city staff, explaining that we're conducting the required audit. We provide a few details about what we're looking for, and everyone will move on."

Irene glanced at her watch. It was past three, far too late to start a thorough search to uncover more checks and bank statements. She stood. "I'll be back on Monday. We will be able to get this sorted out."

Jayne rose as well and held out her hand. "It was nice to meet you. Thank you for your help." Bill and Betty followed suit.

Irene was to the front vestibule when she spotted Lynda Sherry lying in wait. "I wanted to catch you before you left," she stated.

Irene gazed at her impassively. "How can I help you?"

The mayor's smile was probably meant to be warm and confessional, but Irene found it smarmy. "I need you to understand that we're running an experiment on government efficiency. I think you're coming in at a bad time and might leave with the wrong impression."

Irene said, "I'm not concerned about impressions.

My job is to ascertain the facts and to protect taxpayer interests."

Lynda gestured expansively. "We're on the same side. But you're a bureaucrat and I'm a disrupter."

Irene blinked slowly.

"No offense," the mayor continued, "but the government life is cushy. You get raises every year, lots of benefits. And people are sick of paying the tab. It's my job to tighten the belt. And if that means people have to work harder, that's the price we pay." Her eyes lit with fanaticism. "See, it's an experiment. Yes, it *looks* like we're understaffed, but in reality, we're beginning to right-size. Employees are beginning to realize they have to work harder and more efficiently. They've been lazy, and we're now getting to the point where they are starting to realize they are going to have to dig in."

"Mayor Sherry—" Irene tried to interrupt.

"The OA coming in right now is a bad idea. It gives all the workers more ammunition to not do their jobs. They'll spend more time covering their butt against mistakes than getting on with the job." She slapped her hand on the table. "The citizens pay them to work, not to sit around and complain and collect benefits."

"Mayor," Irene said firmly when Lynda paused for breath, "my job is to enforce the laws of Oregon. The City of Lakelynn is required to file an audit every year."

"Yes, but—"

"Checks are missing."

"That's—"

"It doesn't matter what you or anyone says. It's my duty to ensure the citizens of Oregon can trust that their money is spent in a responsible and ethical manner. Until I'm satisfied that I have performed my duties to the best of my ability, my staff and I will stay here."

"So, you're going to be an obstructionist to change."

"I'm going to do my duty."

"Fine. I know where you stand. I'll talk to someone with vision." She stomped back into the offices.

Irene took a few moments in her car to collect herself. She felt shaky. It had been a long, emotional day.

Nervous staff.

Emotional council members.

She remembered her doctor's appointment. Frightened investigator.

Chapter 7

Saturday morning, Irene arrived at the canine agility trial in Brownsville, Oregon. About an hour down I-5 from Salem, the annual trial took place on the hottest days of the year. Luckily, her friend and fellow dog trainer, Sharon Berk, had been able to drive down on Friday to set up her camping and a kenneling area they could share. Irene found Sharon had scored a shady spot close to the river.

The Brownsville Trial was fun because of that river. But having water so close was not without challenges. Last year, Irene's dog, Percy, became so tired from all the playing that she ended up pulling him from the final Sunday events. Now at fourteen, Percy couldn't keep up with the younger dogs, though that didn't stop him from trying. This year, she resolved to try to conserve his energy better.

Percy was a medium-sized mixed breed Irene had adopted from the Marion County Dog Control Shelter ten years ago. Brown and white, with a lithe build that indicated some border collie, he had large ears, big brown eyes, a whip of a tail, and fur that varied in length and texture. In the last few years his muzzle had become increasingly gray, but his eyes were still bright, and his tail thumped a strong beat against his kennel walls as she parked the car. She pulled out the dog's kennel from the car, placed it under the shade tent, then crated him. After unpacking her chair, cooler, and other necessities, she drove her car over to the parking area and walked back to the spot that Sharon had claimed for the last two years and always shared with Irene.

Sharon owned a successful alternative health center called Hands to Soul Healing Center. She had a lovely young blue merle Australian Sheepdog named Mule, who at three was talented but could be opinionated and wild. Sharon's older dog, Sleeve, had died six months ago at the age of sixteen. Irene knew Sharon still missed him.

Sharon stood at one side of the shade tent, examining the setup of the three rings, labeled novice, intermediate and elite. The layout of the show hadn't changed from previous years, so this spot had a decent view of all three rings. The elite ring was the easiest to view from here, but Sharon kept an eye on all of the rings because her dog was in the intermediate level. The best action was usually in the elite ring, though the most humor was usually in the novice ring.

"Have the organizers done a briefing yet?" Irene asked.

"Nope. I think they're still tweaking the courses."

Sharon and Irene were running their dogs in agility, a sport in which a handler directed a dog through an obstacle course where both time and accuracy count. During competition, the dogs ran off leash and there were no toys or food until after the course ends. During training, there were always lots of toys and food. The dogs loved training, but many of them loved the trials, enjoying working the obstacles as fast as possible.

Irene surveyed the rings. The novice ring looked like it had set up a game for points accumulation rather than a strict course, so it was a good way to start the day for the younger dogs. The intermediate ring looked like they were setting up a standard course. The big tournament of the day would end the day in that ring. For the elite ring, the judge had set up a relay course. This was a basic course with a baton hand-off in the middle.

Percy had achieved his agility dog champion title four years ago. Rather than pursue higher titles, Irene had decided to "drop him down" into the older dog class. In this category, the jumps were lowered, there were no spread jumps, and the A-frame was set to a softer slope. All of this made it easier for senior dogs to keep competing. Percy had breezed through the new divisions, quickly picking up more titles.

Like all canine partners, Percy had his strengths and weaknesses. He was great at jumps, tunnels, and weaves, but he found it easier to jump off at the end of a contact than run all the way to the end, something that Irene struggled to teach him.

She walked over to the check-in tent, greeting and chatting with people as she rubbed the tummy of an adorable Basenji puppy named Jamie. "How's Mr. Shy here doing?" she asked his handler.

"Picked up another point last weekend."

"Are you gonna be a champion?" Irene asked Jamie. He looked smug, enjoying the belly rub.

She reached the check-in table and picked up her materials. Another friend went by with her Malinois puppy named Maggie. They were working on Maggie's attention, not allowing the six-month-old to react to all the fascinating sights and sounds.

"So, this is the Mal-a-gator," Irene said, admiring the lithe youngster that she had only seen on social media. "Oh my gosh, she's beautiful."

"I guess I'll keep her," her owner joked. "When are you going to get a puppy?"

Irene continued petting the overjoyed puppy. "Oh, I don't know." It was a topic she didn't like to think about. "I think Percy's still doing okay." She looked up and caught a quick wince from her friend before she hid it.

Releasing the puppy and saying goodbye, Irene walked back to camp. Sharon had reappeared and was chatting about the course that had been put up. Irene heard a whistle in the elite ring, summoning a mob of handlers to the ring. A few moments later, the group listened to the first briefing of the day before they walked the course.

That afternoon, Irene drove home with an exhausted Percy and two qualifying ribbons. There weren't too many days when you got a hundred percent Q rate. Sharon had also had a good day with Mule. She was staying at the campground overnight, sleeping outdoors at the site and the barbequing with the other contestants.

Irene enjoyed her own bed.

****

Irene and Percy arrived back at the trials on Sunday morning, refreshed and ready for more action. She took the dog for a quick walk before reporting for volunteer duty. Percy's events would be mid-morning and afternoon, so she signed up to volunteer to help do things like enter scores, pick up dropped bars, and other jobs that were necessary for making the trial go smoothly.

The standard course always had an A-frame, dog walk, teeter, table, twelve weave poles, tunnel, chute, and jumps. The dogs learned the equipment quickly, but it was maneuvering the different courses that posed the challenges. Dogs had to complete the equipment in a safe manner, touching yellow parts on the end, but also be speedy enough to beat the minimum time. Older dogs like Percy, who were competing in Performance, got extra time.

Irene evaluated the challenging course. The design encouraged dogs to be moving at full speed when approaching the contact obstacles, which increased the likelihood of a missed contact. The weave poles were at a difficult angle for entry, and the table was smack in the middle of an otherwise alluring tunnel.

"That weave pole entrance is hard," she heard over and over again.

"You can't do a front cross there," other competitors agreed.

"Or a rear cross or they pop out."

More opinions could be heard around the edges of the ring.

Irene went to check on Percy before reporting for her stint as a pole setter and found him dozing peacefully in his shady kennel.

An hour later, while the course was being reset for the older dog classes, she took Percy out of his kennel. He stretched luxuriously and happily trotted over to the "exercise" area to do his thing. They took their place in line, tugging on the rope to get warmed up. With two dogs ahead of them, Irene asked Percy to go over the warm-up jump, then helped him do more stretches.

When it was their turn, she told Percy to stand while she walked off a few paces before calling him over the first jump. They quickly tackled the weave pole and tunnels, but Irene saw Percy take a stutter step before the ramp of the A-frame, then dart to the side. This earned a refusal. While competitors are not required to leave the ring after a refusal, Irene pulled up Percy, thanked the judge, and left the ring. Back at the tent, she ran Percy through his cool-down stretches. He yawned in discomfort when Irene massaged his mid back.

"He flinched," Sharon said.

"Yeah," Irene sighed. "I'll pull him for the rest of the day. Do you want to take a look at him?"

Sharon knelt down and endured some face washing before she palpated his spine. "He feels out of alignment," she said quietly. Though Sharon ran a human-centered alternative health care practice, she was a talented practitioner with dogs as well. As she did a quick adjustment, Irene noted that Percy yawned again, a sign of distress.

"I think he pulled something, Irene," Sharon said.

Irene sat and Percy effortlessly leaped up into her lap before she could stop him. He was too big to be a lap dog, but he'd never learned that. Irene would have spared him the jump if she had been a second faster. "I guess that means I'll be taking off for the weekend."

"Guess so," Sharon agreed.

"Do you want me to help you break camp before I go?"

"Nah. I've got it into a routine now."

"Okay. Thanks. Let me buy you lunch this week."

"You're on."

Chapter 8

Irene returned home, unpacked, and took Percy out for a short walk around the neighborhood. He showed no signs of lingering distress from his morning of agility; in fact, he danced under the trees and checked out the squirrels with a predatory gleam in his eyes. But he fell asleep on his favorite dog bed within minutes of returning indoors.

As she fixed herself lunch, she considered what to do with her unexpectedly free afternoon. The stack of books next to a pile of paperwork on the table reminded her what she should do. She sat down at the table with a glass of iced tea and a sandwich and gazed out the window.

MS. Multiple Sclerosis.

In the spring, when she'd gone into the doctor's office for an annual check, she was deemed to be in excellent health. Weight healthy, bloodwork clean, no major bumps or bruises. As she was getting ready to leave the doctor's office, she tried to pick up her purse but because she couldn't close her hand around the handle, ended up dropping it. "I'm such a klutz."

The doctor's brows knitted in a frown. "Does that happen often?"

"Me being a klutz?" Irene rolled her eyes. "More often lately. The other day I couldn't scoot my chair back under my desk."

"Why not?"

Irene made light of it. "My leg kept jerking, and I couldn't coordinate the motions I needed."

The doctor tilted her head. "Anything else out the ordinary? Have your muscles felt tighter than normal? Experiencing any numbness or tingling? Any changes in energy level?"

"What are you saying?"

The doctor shook her head. "Nothing. But it's unusual for someone in their early forties to have trouble grasping objects."

Irene shrugged. "Well, I feel like I've been fighting off a cold or something. Generally tired and achy. That could be anything."

"Yes, it could be." The doctor paused for a moment as if she was considering her approach. "I'd like to do a couple more blood tests to rule a few things out." The doctor smiled. "We haven't spent enough of your insurance company's money this year. Stop by the lab before you leave."

The lab tests came back within normal limits, but as the months progressed, it became more obvious that "it" was wasn't "nothing." Irene began experiencing more bouts of severe muscle spasms. Fatigue dogged her steps, as well as intermittent dizziness. She had fallen several times when one of her legs spasmed and forced her off balance. In the night, she woke up with sudden pain in her legs or abdomen that lasted anywhere from minutes to days.

The doctor sent her to a rheumatologist; more testing indicated she should be at the peak of health. Irene lost more energy. After ruling out many other possibilities, the rheumatologist referred her to Dr.

Mandeville, a neurologist. More tests, including an MRI and a spinal tap for analysis of the fluid.

This last Friday he announced the diagnosis.

"You have multiple sclerosis," he said upon entering the exam room. "The good news is that we're going to diagnose you with relapsing remitting multiple sclerosis. That means that there's a good chance for a slow progression and even periods of normalcy."

She let out the breath she'd been holding. "What do I do now?"

He took a seat on the rolling stool at the side of the exam table. "It's going to be important to take care of yourself. I'm going to prescribe a drug I've had success with. I'll give you the first injection today. The nurse will work out the rest of the schedule when we set you up for follow-up appointments."

Irene panicked. "Why do I have to take medication if it's the slow progressing kind?"

"This drug and other medications have been shown to reduce the number of relapses and occurrence of new lesions. They may also slow disease progression. It's a standard course of treatment to start a medication once the diagnosis has been confirmed."

He studied her face for another moment before he said, "I'd like to recommend a support group and some exercise classes. Twenty years ago, people didn't know much about the condition; there weren't any drugs or therapies. We used to tell people not to exercise or move too much. Now, we're in the 'move it or lose it' mode."

Irene nodded, trying to control her breathing. "My friend told me she read yoga can help?"

"It's hard to find the right class, but yoga can be helpful," he said. "Anything to keep your muscles from deteriorating. That's what will put you in a wheelchair."

"Does that mean I can continue my other activities? Dog agility?"

"It's possible you can continue with it, but you need to take care of yourself. Your body is not the same as it was. It's slower to heal. It's more reactive to damage. From what you've told me about agility, and what I've seen from you, I'm not sure it's a long-term lifestyle possibility."

Irene nodded, blinking back tears.

Dr. Mandeville laid a comforting hand on her arm. "Irene, I know this is hard. You have so many possibilities for keeping healthy, and more are being developed all the time. Go to the support group. Talk to your family. Figure out what's most important and then make some decisions."

She nodded again. "I'm taking the rest of the day off, so I'll have some time to process this."

"That's good."

"I'm not sure what to do. I've read about next steps, but—"

"It's a lot to process," he finished for her.

****

Irene had known MS was a possible diagnosis before Friday's visit. She had gone online to research her symptoms as well as diagnostic testing options and learned enough to understand MS is an unpredictable disease of the central nervous system that disrupts the flow of information within the brain, and between the brain and body. Women were more likely than men to get it, and the rate is twice as high in the Pacific Northwest.

She had shared her concerns with Sharon, who had

amassed a huge collection of literature for Irene to read, as well as found alternative treatments.

Shifting her attention to the current moment, Percy snoozing in his bed, she picked up her sandwich and flipped open the first of the books Sharon had given her. She needed to face facts and start thinking about lifestyle changes.

Her phone rang. She checked the caller, sighed, and answered. "Hi, Angie."

"Hey. Thanks for agreeing to babysit on Friday."

"I always enjoy spending time with the boys."

"I wanted to talk to you about making it a regular thing."

Irene lapsed into silence.

"Jason and I have been seeing a counselor, and she thinks we need to spend more time together. We thought it might be easier to have a regular date night, and so I wanted to see if I could get you to babysit on Fridays." Angie was in pitch mode. Her voice sounded eerily like their mother's.

Irene said nothing.

"I know you're busy and you can't regularly do anything late. If Fridays won't work, maybe you could take the boys one weekday evening. Go hiking, feed them dinner, watch a movie, and then we'd be back. Easy." Angie had shifted from pitch to persuasion.

Irene took a deep breath. "What evening were you thinking of?"

"If you can't do Friday…"

"I don't think that will work."

"How about Wednesday? A break in the middle of the week. Jason and I would do something simple and be back by eight or nine." A note of pleading entered her voice.

"Did you ask Jennifer?" Their mother insisted on being called by her given name.

Angie gave a small huff. "Well, I would, but you know how she is. She'd never let the boys get into trouble, but she'd probably call half the time and beg out, saying she has a showing or something."

Irene studied her hands. "Angie, I don't know that I can do it every week."

"Please, Irene. Jason and I need this. The counselor thinks we need regular time together to be a couple."

"You could ask Jennifer to do it every other week. Or hire a babysitter."

There was a short, accusatory silence. "Why can't you do this?" Angie said coolly.

Sitting at the table stacked with books about her medical condition, Irene thought about confessing everything to her sister. Instead, she said, "We are short-staffed at work and I'm putting in extra hours all the time. You're not the only one with a life." This came out with more accusation than she intended.

"And you're not the only one with a job, but I *am* the only one with children."

"That you are asking *me* to take care of."

"Fine." Angry silence crackled between them.

Irene took a deep breath. "Angie, I can commit to every other week. But right now, I don't think I can do more than that."

"I'll talk to Jennifer and see if she can take them."

"Okay. Text me the next few dates and I'll put them on my calendar."

"Put down Wednesdays," Angie said carelessly.

"Text me the dates," Irene said coolly.

Angie hung up.

Irene made herself another cup of tea and went back to reading. She didn't know how long it was until her phone rang again, startling her. The call was identified as Jennifer. Irene toyed with ignoring the call, but she knew it wouldn't improve her mother's mood. Jennifer was more than capable of re-dialing every five minutes until receiving a response.

"Hello, Jennifer."

"Why can't you take the boys every week?" her mother demanded.

"Because I'm busy."

"It's the least you could do. It's not like you have children. Or even a husband."

"Why don't you take them?" Irene countered.

"They wouldn't have any fun with me," Jennifer said smoothly. "Besides, you never know when I'll have to do a showing."

"Right."

Jennifer ignored the sarcasm. "I was going to call you anyway. I had to let my accountant go. This is the second one in a year."

Irene knew where this was going. "She wasn't an accountant; she was a bookkeeper."

"I want you to take over our account."

"I have a job. And I'm not a bookkeeper."

"I don't understand what difference that makes."

Rather than engage, Irene let the silence drag.

"Why can't you help me out?" Jennifer pouted. "It's a part-time job."

"No, Jennifer, it's a full-time job that you try to squeeze into a half-time job."

"I'm sure you could do it," Jennifer said

persuasively, sounding like Angie.

"But I'm not going to," Irene said firmly.

"What do you expect me to do?" Jennifer whined.

"Hire a full-time bookkeeper and pay a fair wage," Irene suggested.

"I pay a fair wage. It's just adding and subtracting."

"Do it yourself, then."

Jennifer went silent. Both of them knew she loathed doing the books, though there had been periods of time when she had done it to make ends meet. In high school, Irene had been naïve and earnest enough to try to help her, but Jennifer was unable to admit even the simplest error, and the sessions had quickly escalated into a shouting match. It had added to the stress of an already difficult period in their lives.

"Irene, I need your help."

"I can ask around and put out the word, but that's all I will do. I won't work for you. I won't take on another job."

"So, you are refusing to help me." If Irene had left her without water stranded on the side of a desert highway, Jennifer's tone could not have been more accusatory.

Irene took a deep breath. "Why did you let your bookkeeper go?"

"Well… actually, she quit."

Obviously, she had quit. Jennifer would have worked her like a dog and paid her the lowest amount possible. "Is there some reason why you can't pay a bookkeeper the going rate? Is the business in trouble again?"

"Don't be ridiculous. Business is booming. It's silly to pay more than I have to."

"You also used to do your own cleaning and staging. Now you pay for those things to be done. Why can't you accept you need to pay for this?" Irene said reasonably.

"The clients don't see this."

"They do. Every time you can't settle on time or there's an error on their estimate."

"That's a different program," Jennifer said dismissively.

"It doesn't have to be," Irene pointed out. "Hire a qualified professional!" Irene shifted screens on her phone and searched for an article. "I'm sending you an article I read the other day about integrating accounting and closing software."

Unmoved, Jennifer said, "But you won't come work for me."

"No, I won't."

Jennifer hung up.

Chapter 9

Monday morning, Irene arrived at the office early, determined to talk to her boss, sort out her schedule, and tackle her in-box. She dropped her bag onto her desk chair and made her way to John Fisher's office.

John was at his desk, as she had expected him to be. Born in New England, John had never made an attempt to mimic the more relaxed West Coast work ethos. He wore a tie and jacket nearly every day; he arrived at the office at six a.m. freshly showered from a brisk five-mile run. While he occasionally had a business lunch, Irene could count the number of times she had seen him leave the office before five p.m. Though he was driven and abrupt, Irene liked him as an associate and respected him as a boss.

She knocked on the doorway. "John, can I talk to you?"

He grunted in acknowledgement, intent on finishing the email he was working on. Irene took a seat at his desk, closing the door behind her.

She closed her eyes, guilt swamping her as she spoke. "John, I know the timing isn't ideal, but I need to take some medical leave."

Irritation crossed his face. With an aggrieved sigh, he pulled up a calendar. "Candace isn't due back from maternity leave for another three weeks. The postings for the replacement auditors went out last week, so it will be the end of the month before we even get to interviews."

"John, this isn't a matter of some vacation. I'm having some health issues and need time to get them sorted out. I'd like to take a month off."

"Obviously, if you need medical leave, you have it available," he said after a moment. "But the workload can't accommodate a month-long vacation from a senior investigator."

Irene studied him. "We've talked about my taking time off over the summer."

"That was before—"

"John, it's always something. It's always going to be something. I was burned out even before this medical stuff. I need some time off, soon."

He scowled at her. "I'm not stopping you from taking medical leave."

"I have so much vacation time that I'm in danger of losing it unless I use it."

"I'll write you a variance."

"I don't want a variance; I want the time off you promised."

"Irene, I'm sorry we're busy. I'll work with you to flex your schedule. But we are short staffed, and I can't approve a month-long vacation. I don't have the staff." He examined the calendar still on his screen. "Ask for the time off you need in September. I'll approve it."

She stood to leave. "Thank you."

****

Peter Hampton and Irene loaded their laptops into the car, slamming the doors in unison. Irene had dressed for the day in a black fitted no-iron dress shirt, white skirt, dressy sandals, and a chunky belt. He had chosen gray pants, a peach shirt, and a paisley jacket that combined the two colors. His bow tie and pocket square accented everything perfectly, as usual. Peter's latest boyfriend worked in a trendy northwest Portland men's clothing boutique. This combination of two great loves had kept Peter in seventh heaven, though his credit card might die of the trauma. Irene tossed him the keys. After stopping to grab a coffee, they were navigating north.

"So," Peter began. "Who done it?"

Irene smiled. "I'm not sure yet."

"I heard the mayor was a handful."

Irene rolled her eyes. "You don't need to watch her; you need to wear earplugs."

While Peter wasn't Irene's assistant, she had taken him under her wing. He was detail-oriented, meticulous, and brilliant, which made him a great asset on any investigation. As an assistant criminal financial investigator, Peter was at least one rung below her on the professional ladder. While some of that was attributable to age, Irene knew his real trouble was soft skills; Peter had a tendency to drop his poker face. He had a hair-pin trigger and sporadically questionable people skills. Even with those drawbacks, he was an excellent accountant. He and Irene worked well together, and they shared coffee at least once a week.

They arrived in Lakelynn to find Rusty Barrett waiting for them in the lobby. He shook Peter's hand, then Irene's and gestured for them to follow as he made his way back to the large conference room on the side of the building. "I've got the other auditors set up in here. I assumed you'd want to join them?"

"That's fine," Irene said.

The room contained a team of five private auditors, each with at least one computer hooked up to a central hub that contained power, internet, and printing.

After introductions, they set up at the end of the long conference table. Listening to the tasks the senior auditor assigned his team, Irene knew they were taking the same steps she would have when starting an audit—focusing on trial balances and understanding the personnel and departments they would be dealing with. One of the workers was assigned exclusively to testing records. It was a basic set-up, designed to discover if the city had represented their fiscal position and procedures accurately. They would look at how things were done versus how they were supposed to be done, searching for discrepancies.

Irene's plan was to allow the private audit to commence while she and Peter focused on cash handling and banking. Their job was to discover if someone had their hand in the cookie jar. They would start interviewing staff to document who handled money, mail, checks, and assorted financial tasks through interviews.

Looking over her list, she felt concern. The Lakelynn finance department was dangerously understaffed. Most cities this size had around seven full-time finance employees, often including at least two certified CPA's; Lakelynn had five finance employees, none of which currently held a CPA license. Based on her study of the organizational chart, too many people had access to too many parts of the process.

Minutes later, Peter interrupted her thoughts. "Irene? Are you sure we're only looking for a missing check or two?"

"What do you mean?"

"There are lots of checks missing from the

sequence."

Irene walked over to look at his screen which contained a spreadsheet listing checks issued over the last three years. Groups of checks were highlighted, with no information about payee or amount listed.

"Are they marking it wasted?" she asked. It was best practice to document what happened to each check. Misprinted checks were marked "wasted," then destroyed by city staff. Stopped checks were marked and destroyed by the bank.

"They're not marking it as anything. There are gaps each month."

"Did they give us the unused check stock?"

Peter riffled through a ream of checks. "Yes, and there's a lot of it. A bunch was placed into the printer backward. They kept it, but didn't document the numbers in the system."

"Okay, we'll add it to the list." She looked at her own screen. "It's been about three weeks since the last check run. See what you can find."

"Huh," Peter grunted.

Chapter 10

Irene went down to the basement, where Rusty worked with Betty Hacher and Kathy Nicols in the file room. As she approached, she heard Betty's grating voice. Betty and Rusty turned toward Irene when she entered, but Kathy remained bent over her work.

"How's it going?" Irene asked.

"Slow, but I think we're making progress." Rusty looked around. "We've put out a rush order for more cabinets and files."

"I've been requesting those for months," Betty accused, glaring at Irene was though it was all her fault.

"I know," Rusty said in a soothing tone. "We should have taken your advice earlier."

Irene hid a smile. "Rusty, do you have time for a quick meeting?"

"Sure. We're getting the worst of it cleared up."

"Great." Irene turned to Betty. "I'd like to talk to you after I finish with Rusty, if that's okay."

"Do I have a choice?" she snapped.

"Of course. Let me know when is convenient. I'd like to get to you soon." Irene turned to Kathy. "Can I schedule you today as well?"

Kathy looked startled, but Betty spoke before she could answer. "I guess we can talk after you talk to Rusty."

"Excellent. Kathy, can I put in you in line?"

She hesitated. "I guess."

"Okay. Betty, I'll see you in about an hour. Kathy, we'll speak after lunch."

Rusty escorted Irene to his office and closed the door before sitting down. Irene reviewed her notes. He'd attended the University of Washington and graduated with a degree in general business. After college he went to work for a series of non-profits before starting a career at the small eastern Washington town of Connell whose population was over five thousand. He worked his way up to city administrator during the course of his fifteen-year career with Connell before accepting this position in Lakelynn three months ago. His resumé and online professional profile painted a portrait of a competent manager, if not one striving to set the world on fire.

"So, how's it going?" Irene asked to break the ice.

Rusty breathed out. "The city is in the middle of a state audit; the file room is a mess; and my chief financial officer is spitting mad. It's been better."

"I can imagine. Have you found any additional check stock?"

He shook his head. "We haven't found anything other than what we gave you on Friday."

"Beginning an audit can be overwhelming," Irene soothed. "You and your team will have to find balance sheets, bylaws, policies, org charts…you name it."

"I've given those to the private auditors. And they've asked for more." He met Irene's gaze. "I suppose you'll need a copy, too."

Irene shook her head. "We can get them from the audit team."

"I didn't ask on Friday. How will your investigation be different from the auditors?"

"A standard audit is not necessarily looking for fraud. They want to make sure the city's financial position is stated correctly, that the money in the bank is there. The buildings are theirs, not owned by the bank.

"The OA team will do a modified forensic audit. We'll approach the audit with the mindset that something already is wrong. It's not uncommon to go into an audit and know what the fraud was and who did it. It's my job to find out who had committed the fraud, how they did it, then present the findings to a jury."

"So, you're like the police?"

Irene shook her head. "More like an expert witness. And as an OA auditor, my focus is going to be even more varied. Most of the time, when the audit division comes in, we're simply enforcement. Sometimes we investigate. Occasionally, we have to work with the fraud prosecutors to file charges. We have to balance enforcement with sleuthing."

"Do you really think something is wrong?" Rusty asked.

"We already know something is wrong," Irene said gently. "The city is two years behind on its audits. The missing check stock only hastened our arrival." She stopped to take another sip of coffee. "Is the organization stream becoming more obvious?"

Rusty shook his head. "It looks like things were in good shape until about two years ago. Then things started to pile up instead of being filed. Like the audits."

"Why do you think that happened?"

"The finance team was in transition. The former financial manager left suddenly. The former mayor was generating attention. No one was steering the ship."

"Wasn't Betty acting as the finance manager?"

Rusty studied his hands. "I'm not sure about the timing, but we can assume she was somewhere in the mix."

Irene studied him. "When did Betty become the finance director?"

"I haven't been able to find the exact date," he admitted with a frown. "It took a couple of months before they offered her the position."

"Do you think that's significant?" Irene clarified. "That it took time for her to move into the position?"

"I think if they thought she would have been a good fit, they would have offered her the job right after the previous director left," Rusty paused. "But it's possible that other things distracted everyone."

"What other things?"

Rusty blew out a breath. "From what I understand, after the previous mayor's actions hit the front page, everything was in turmoil for several months. Then there was the election of the new mayor, who immediately made drastic staffing cuts. She froze all hiring and requested every department to put forward a twenty-five percent budget reduction."

Irene nodded. She had read the details in newspaper reports.

"Lynda is the one who hired me, so you'd think I'd be singing her praises. Instead, I'm putting out her fires. When she hired me, she was so charming. She talked about wanting better accountability for the voters and cutting waste. I was excited to take the job."

"Why did you decide to relocate?" Irene inquired.

"I wanted a change. I had been filling out applications. I figured if I got a job offer, I could make a decision then. Lynda's enthusiasm convinced me it would be a good move."

Irene looked at her notes. "I thought the entire council hired the city manager."

"I had a second interview with some of the council members. Jayne Tanaka wasn't there because her husband was battling cancer."

"So, it was—" Irene consulted her notes again. "—Lynda Sherry, Bill Henley, and Robert Austin."

Rusty nodded.

"When we first met," Irene said, "you said you weren't sure if you were interim or permanent. Does the lack of the full council hiring process have anything to do with your uncertainty?"

Rusty took another long breath and leaned back in his chair. It was a few moments before he spoke. "I asked a lawyer look over my contract last week and he told me that unless the full council approved my contract, it could be argued that the contract was never fully ratified. I didn't know that. Plus, in the last three months I don't think a week has gone by where Lynda hasn't told me I'm fired. You saw her on Friday."

Irene remembered the mayor's dramatic entrance. "That sounds stressful."

"The first few times, I thought she was joking, that she didn't mean it. But what I've learned since then is that she'll do anything to get her way."

"What does that look like?"

"I never believed I would say this about a real-life person, but she's... devious. Sneaky. She starts off charming, but she'll push until she gets what she wants. And anyone who gets in her way doesn't last long."

Irene nodded, encouraging him to continue.

"For example, last month she got into it with the

head of the parks commission, which is a volunteer position. All the commission does is make recommendations on city policy. In that instance, he came to a meeting to present a study on the city's swimming pool, which is in need of renovation. Cut and dried stuff. It wasn't a surprise to anyone."

"What happened?" Irene asked.

"Lynda found out about the recommendation. She made an emergency change of agenda, which prevented him from presenting the report. A few days later, the parks chair turned in his resignation and sent a nasty letter into the newspaper, talking about the city being obstructionist and endangering the public."

"What happened then?"

"When I asked Lynda about it, she said, 'good riddance' and made a motion for the council to dismantle the commission. That hasn't gone through yet, but it's typical of her my way or the highway approach to people. She'll do whatever it takes to get anyone who disagrees with her out."

"So, you don't feel able to speak up," Irene concluded.

"Are you kidding? If I cross her, she'll go out of her way to trash me to any other potential employer. Don't even get me started on her 'experiment theory' of government. I thought she was talking about a few cuts, some right-sizing. She honestly means to remove any kind of governmental regulatory power. No government. That's her dream. She doesn't care about schools, police, or anything else."

Chapter 11

Back in the conference room, Irene made notes on her computer before checking in with Peter. "Anything new?"

"I've determined most of their check stock is either here or has been processed," he said. "There is one check that I can't find and about six that haven't been cashed yet."

"Okay. Keeping going. Have the bank statements come in?"

Peter rolled his eyes and opened his mouth to speak when Betty Hacher stomped into the conference room. Once again, she was under-dressed in a wide-strapped tank top and jeans. "Here are the statements from the bank," she grumbled, tossing a heap of unopened envelopes in Peter's direction. Impassively, he and Irene turned to study it. "All the statements are online now," she continued, hackles clearly raised. "We print them off. I don't understand why you care about what the bank sends." Betty's raspy alto didn't create an effective wail, but she made up for it in sheer volume.

Peter carefully gathered the statements. "Thank you."

As Betty's face turned red, Irene stood. Keeping her face neutral while studying the other woman's expression and body language, she said, "I'm glad you came in. Do you have time to meet with me now?"

Betty clearly dug for control, but after a moment she nodded.

"Great," Irene said. "Would your office be acceptable?"

A few minutes later, they were seated across from each other with Betty's cluttered desk between them. Like the file room, there were stacks of paper everywhere. Betty made belligerent eye contact with Irene, her jaw set, her arms folded in a stiff, defensive posture.

While giving them both a moment and doing a deep breathing exercise she hoped Betty would subconsciously mimic, Irene recalled her notes. Betty Hacher was a career finance professional. She had worked as a bookkeeper before going back to school to get her master's degree. After graduating, she worked for an accountant doing audits before moving into municipal finance. Until a couple of years ago she maintained a CPA license, but had let it lapse. This wasn't an unreasonable step; Betty had to be nearing retirement age. Between regular recertification requirements and the costs for the associated training, the fees could amount to several thousand dollars. If Betty figured she was near retirement and her current position didn't require a CPA, Irene could see her quietly letting her commission drop.

After a few moments, Irene could see her gamble had worked. Betty sat back in her chair, taking a deep breath. One hand stayed close to her side, but the other rested on the desk.

Irene smiled. "I'd like to start out by apologizing. I should have let you know that part of my job is to prevent and uncover waste, fraud, and abuse. My questions can seem personal, but they aren't. You understand that, don't you?"

"Yes. But I feel like you're not listening to me."

Irene nodded. "I'm listening now."

Betty scowled. "What I'm saying is why do the originals matter? We can download a copy from the bank at any time."

"Who downloads and prints the statements?"

A look of concern crossed Betty's face. "It doesn't matter."

Trying to look sympathetic, Irene nodded. "Probably not. But it's one more piece of the puzzle. We usually add it to the report as a matter of record."

"Well...sometimes I do, but most of the time it's Kathy Nicols, the assistant finance director."

Irene made a note, then looked up again. "So, you've been here quite a long time. Tell me about who I'll be working with. What are their strengths and weaknesses?"

She blinked. "I'm not a gossip."

"Of course not. I'm trying to get a sense of the office. It strikes me as having a lot of...big personalities."

Betty grunted. "Too big."

"Right. And obviously everyone is doing the best they can," Irene said smoothly, "but I'm sure there must be areas where you think improvements could be made."

"We're so understaffed," Betty whined.

Irene continued her note taking. "What kind of problems has that created?"

This gave Betty confidence and within moments she was creating a picture of an office where the only person who did their job was her. Irene kept on nodding, encouraging Betty to keep going. "But the mayor keeps interfering," Betty burst out at the end of a tirade about the human resources department.

"Interfering how?"

"Well…like, last week she wanted us to pay a vendor without a contract. I told her she couldn't do that without a formal request for proposal, but she said it was an emergency. When I asked for the emergency declaration, she sent Rusty down to tell me to pay the vendor."

"Did Rusty interfere?"

"No. He found the correct documentation and sent it to me."

Irene nodded. "What was that vendor's name?"

Betty looked alarmed but named the vendor of safety equipment.

"What else would you like to tell me?"

For some reason, venting about the mayor took the wind out of Betty's sails. She looked blank, like no one had ever asked her for so many opinions before. The silence dragged on for a moment.

"So let me ask you some questions," Irene said mildly. "Where do you think the city is wasting money?"

"We aren't!" Betty exploded passionately.

"You don't see any unnecessary purchases? What about the invoice you were talking about?"

"Well, we did need that fire equipment; we just hadn't put out the RFP. Request for proposals," Betty explained hastily.

"She, the mayor, asked you to bend the rules."

Betty nodded vigorously. "And I don't do that."

"I can see that. Do you think the city has any vulnerabilities?"

"No. I think we run a tight ship."

"Would you tell me if you did think there were any problems?"

They locked gazes for a moment. "Like I said, I'm not a gossip."

Irene decided to change the subject. "Okay. Let's talk about the basics. What are the steps to take before you approve an invoice for payment?"

Chapter 12

Returning to the conference room after her interview with Betty Hacher, Irene noted the audit team was still remarkably focused. As Peter moved over a small mountain of bank statements, she sat to follow up on emails that had come in during her absence. A few minutes later, Peter looked up from his task.

She smiled at him. "How's it going?"

"I'm making progress." He leaned toward Irene. "The accounting team is starting to make some noise, but I'd say it's going better than expected."

"Let's hope some training and effective management can sort them out," Irene murmured.

Peter didn't look convinced. "What have you found out?"

Irene thought for a minute. "I was going to go over and get a coffee at the place across the street. Do you want to join me?"

Peter understood what she wasn't saying and agreed to join her.

They made their way across the street and ordered their drink, then went to sit on a bench under a tree, out of the crowd and relatively quiet. "The finance director told me the mayor had tried to push some payments through without contracts."

Peter took a sip of coffee.

"And the city manager described the mayor as petty

and vindictive."

Another sip. Finally, he said. "That's interesting about the contracts. The accounting group said they're consistently late about closing the books. I also heard them say the city makes more than the average number of journal entries and last-minute check runs."

"What's the hold-up on the closings?" Irene asked.

"I haven't heard, but it was mentioned in their last audit."

"The one from two years ago?"

Peter nodded. "The target date is the fifteenth of the month. They add between five and ten days to that every time."

"Interesting."

They sat for a while before Irene broke the silence, getting to her real point. "I'm concerned that any report we make is going to go in one ear and out the other."

Peter shrugged. "It's always a danger."

She sighed and rolled her coffee cup in her hands. "This is going to go sideways."

Peter nodded.

****

Irene and Peter returned to the city hall and joined the audit team for a quick lunch. The group chatted amiably, occasionally launching into an amusing audit anecdote or revealing reconciliation report with good humor. Irene joined in with the others but kept turning the information over in her head.

No auditor could fix a broken system. Auditors gave opinions, reports, and advice; if the people hearing the advice didn't want to listen, not much could be done. For all the effort and focus, audits only made a difference if someone was willing to take the steps to fix the problem.

Irene was concerned about the publicity and politics that shrouded this investigation. Auditors were almost never cast as heroes in the headlines. Lynda Sherry and her ambitions for the role of governor posed a threat. It was possible the consequences of an unflattering audit could become a pawn in the mayor's ambitions. The audit results would become a secondary annoyance, a scapegoat for the issue in the spotlight.

After lunch, Irene met with Kathy Nicols, Assistant Finance Director, in a small conference room down the hall from the auditors. According to her research, Kathy had graduated from college in Arizona and stayed to work in Phoenix for seven years before moving north to Reno. Her move to Oregon coincided with her acceptance of the position in Lakelynn. While she did not have an accounting degree, her experience showed a steady progression up the finance ladder. With over twenty years of financial experience, she was an important player in the Lakelynn ecosystem.

Irene smiled at Kathy in an attempt to build a rapport. The woman was clearly anxious as evidenced by the constant twisting of her wedding ring around her finger. "Thanks for meeting with me. I've been running around all morning. I haven't had much time to talk to anyone."

"It's been busy," Kathy agreed. "I feel like I've been directing traffic." She twisted her wedding ring.

Irene nodded. "Sometimes, I feel like I need a bullhorn. How long have you been at the city?"

"Since 2011," Kathy answered. "I was hired by the last finance director to do accountants payable." Her hands had slowed their tugging on the ring.

"When did you get promoted to assistant director?"

"January."

"So, Betty promoted you?"

"Yes. But I wasn't her first choice." Kathy's voice was perfectly neutral.

"Oh," Irene said. She looked down at the list of city personnel. To her eyes, no one else looked equally qualified. "Did they take outside candidates?"

"No." Kathy took a breath. "Betty's first choice decided to retire, after the mayor was elected, of course."

"And you were offered the position instead?"

"Yes." The word was said flatly. Irene couldn't tell if she had any particular opinions about her promotion.

Irene studied her for a moment. "Do you know why the OA is here?"

She swallowed hard. "I heard a check went missing and now they are worried about embezzlement." Her flat, matter-of-fact demeanor was gone, replaced by nerves and fears.

"That's what got me here today," Irene agreed. "The city hasn't filed an audit for two years. I'm hearing rumors about the school construction project being compromised. Things don't look like they are going in the right direction." Kathy nodded, but her face didn't register the same concern as the mention of the missing check stock. Irene studied her for another moment. "What kind of problems do you think the auditor will uncover?"

Kathy gave a tiny shrug.

Irene smiled again. "I've never interviewed anyone who couldn't think of something that could be done better."

Kathy sighed. "I'm nervous. I don't want the city to get in trouble."

"I understand. What about the filing? When did that get so bad?"

"Oh." She relaxed again. "That was a few years ago. Homer and the last finance director couldn't stand each other. They had some kind of argument about the files, and from then on, we were supposed to do our own filing."

"Did you?"

"Well, most of us dumped it on our assistant. Then, when she left, the mayor wouldn't let Betty rehire the position. She said we should be doing our own filing."

Irene nodded. "So why didn't you?"

"Who says I didn't?" Kathy retorted defiantly.

Irene smiled. "I meant 'you' collectively. I'm sure you, in particular, always did your own filing."

Kathy warmed up enough to give Irene a conspiratorial smile. "Well, honestly, Betty told us not to do it so the mayor would see we didn't have time."

"And you didn't want to get between the mayor and Betty."

Kathy rolled her eyes. "Would you?"

Irene chuckled. "Fair enough." She checked her notes. "I see that isn't the only position that hasn't been filled."

Kathy nodded. "We've lost an AP and AR position. Excuse me," she said quickly. "Accountings Payable and Accounting Receivable." She rolled her eyes. "My boyfriend hates it when I lapse into accounting speak."

Irene nodded. "My family does, too. But I know what AP and AR stand for. Those two positions used to be two full time equivalents each? How is it going without them?"

"Betty and I have been pitching in to get the end-of-the-month reporting done. But that means we can't do all our work."

"What is not getting done?"

Kathy looked down and started twirling her wedding ring again. "Obviously the audits."

Irene nodded sympathetically. "Obviously."

"We haven't been able to get out the board report the last couple of months. Ms. Tanaka is the only one who asked about it."

Irene made a note. "What did she say?"

"She stopped by a couple days after the last board meeting and asked about it. I overheard her talking to Betty before they went into her office."

"Was Ms. Tanaka upset?"

Kathy thought about it. "No. Maybe? Mostly impatient. But not with us," she said hastily. "Just…in a hurry."

"Do you think the understaffing has led to cutting corners in separation of duties?"

"We do our best." Kathy said, defensive again.

"I'm sure you do," Irene said. "But it's fair to say you can't do everything?"

Kathy looked down at her hands. "That's fair."

Irene decided to take another tack. "Rusty is concerned about the missing check stock. What do you think about that?"

"The filing is a mess," she said with a shrug, her face relaxing again. "It's probably there somewhere."

Irene studied her for another moment. She had expected Kathy to be more forthcoming; someone with her experience would have had prior experience with audits. Finally, she flipped to the next page of her legal pad. "Tell me about the city's approval process for checks."

Kathy nodded, happy to have something factual to talk about. "The program managers approve invoices for various projects. Usually, they have worked with the contracting department to get the agreements executed, but occasionally they use a city card or work with contracts to use a price agreement. Once the invoice has been approved, it comes to our department for entry into the system. In the past, we've had two positions for that, but now we're down to one."

Irene looked down at the organization chart, following along. "Christina Johnson, right?"

Kathy nodded. "She's good with details and does her best to keep up. Once everything is entered, the paperwork moves to my desk. I'll review the expenses, make sure we have money in the account to cover it, then run the checks. From there, Betty will look everything over, sign or stamp as necessary, and give everything back to Christine for filing and mailing."

Irene nodded. "That's a lot of back and forth. Are there any checks or payments that don't come through Christina?"

Kathy nodded. "Contract payments are generated in the accounting system. For example, the homeless shelter gets an EFT—electronic funds transfer—the first of every month. Betty takes care of those."

Irene made a note. "Who reviews those payments?"

Kathy looked confused. "They're regular payments."

"Surely, they change sometimes?" Irene asked. "Or contracts stop? Vendors move?"

Kathy thought about it for a moment. "I'm sure that happens. But the contracting department is in charge of keeping track of the vendors. And the software keeps track of when the payments are supposed to end." She brightened. "I guess I forgot to mention that with our software, several people have to sign off on the contracts and the payments in the system before the EFT is generated. Betty is sort of the last step there."

"So, you're printing the checks and Betty's making the EFT's. Does anyone check her work?"

"No. After everyone has signed off, she can't change anything."

Silence fell as Irene made some notes on her legal pad. "You mentioned a stamp."

"We have a stamp for payments under one thousand dollars; Betty has to sign for amounts over that. If the check is for more than $10,000, Rusty has to cosign."

"Who was in possession of the stamp?" Irene asked.

"Betty has it."

"What did the stamp have on it?"

"It's the mayor's signature. We put it on everything, but when the amounts are over the limit, we add signatures."

Irene finished her notes. "Okay. Thank you, Kathy. I think I have enough."

Cautiously, Kathy rose from her seat. "I hope I was helpful. I'm nervous."

"You told me plenty."

****

Irene and Peter discussed the day's findings as they drove back to Salem. This time, she drove, and he reviewed his notes.

"I've been trying to match their list of contracts to payees, then to checks," Peter told her. "There are a few contracts either haven't been finalized or aren't on the list. I recognize some—Metro Emergency Service, Chief Supplies."

"Those are standard vendors," Irene mused. "Why haven't they finalized these contracts?"

"I can't find any information. Rusty said the contracts were old but still valid. When I pressed, he said he'd get them to me by the end of the week."

"Follow up. They may be using the state's price agreements, but it's worth a look."

"A few could be the names of individuals," Peter warned her.

"Well, it's too early to jump to conclusions. How did the auditors do?"

"The city recorder straightened out the file room, and now they have all the bank statements. The balance sheets are finished. The lead auditor told me he'd like to set up a meeting with us before the end of the week."

Irene turned on her blinker to move into the right lane. "Well, that doesn't sound promising." She thought for a moment. "Find out if they can meet with us on Friday."

"Will do." Peter said, returning the spreadsheet of vendors to his file.

"Don't spend a lot of time on the contracts. The auditors will sort it out. But search those names you don't immediately recognize. See what comes up. We might find something to focus on."

"I already did that for a few," he admitted. "Most appear to be small business owners. There's one that's odd though." He took out the spreadsheet again. "Willamette Falls Consulting."

"Why is that odd?

"There's no listing for Willamette Falls Consulting.

I ran an online search under several different engines. Nothing. Nada."

"Hmmm." Irene thought for a moment. "That's a generic business name."

Peter nodded in agreement.

She continued. "It's too soon to tell, but it would be nice for once to be dealing with someone who's smart enough not to make the checks out in their own name."

Peter laughed. "Dare to dream."

Chapter 13

Wednesday evening, Irene reported to Angie's house shortly before six p.m. She had packed a small bag with jeans and a T-shirt for her babysitting duties. Knowing Angie, she had also put in a few overnight essentials, though she desperately hoped she'd not to have to use them.

Irene rang the bell and listened to the chaotic noises of Angie and Jason trying to get the boys situated. Angie pulled the door back, revealing her elaborately casual outfit.

"Are you going to a barn raising?" Irene asked skeptically.

Angie was dressed in a checkered top that hugged every curve, skin-tight jeans, cowboy boots, and a straw hat. Her elaborately enhanced blonde hair fell in careless waves around her shoulders. Her makeup, as always, was flawless, but Irene noted her eyeliner was thicker and the overall color palette was brighter. Her jewelry was big, bright, and plentiful.

Like Irene, Angie was slightly above average height, but there were few similarities beyond that. Irene had dark brown hair cut in an easy-maintenance cut; Angie was a blond who regularly played up her color and style to match the latest trends. Irene had attractive, even features; Angie had done some modeling and commercials in her early twenties. While Irene's figure was fit and flexible, her sister possessed an hourglass figure that ensured she would never buy her own drinks.

"No," Angie laughed merrily. "We're going line dancing. There's this great new place that opened up at the center."

Her husband, Jason, came up behind her. He was also costumed as a cowboy, though he had opted for a button-down, two-tone shirt complete with fringe. Like his wife, Jason was an extremely handsome man. Tall, blond, and charming, he exuded a bonhomie machismo that made him easy to like and always in the top five salespeople at his dealership. "Irene, right on time as usual. One of these days, something will happen, and you'll be a couple minutes late."

Irene took a subtle, but deep breath. She told herself that Jason didn't mean to make it sound like she didn't have a life. She wasn't sure she believed it. Before she could respond, Dave and Mike descended the stairs and ran into her arms.

"Hi, Aunt Ree." Dave had been unable to fully pronounce Irene for a few years, so he had shortened it to "Ree," and the name stuck. Both boys were the image of their father, but their personalities were radically different from Jason, Angie, and each other.

Dave was nine and Irene had him down with a future in the sciences or engineering. He always wanted to know how things worked and why. Mike was six and spent his time evenly divided between catching up with Dave and discovering the world. For Christmas, Irene had purchased a GPS unit that they could use for geocaching, and they regularly explored different areas looking for the hidden finds. Dave was in charge of the GPS unit and logs; Mike took the lead on exploring every available area. Irene was content to be the supervisor, chauffeur, and phone owner.

"Where are we going today?" Mike demanded.

"We made an electric propeller car today," Dave told her, holding up the little car made of cardboard with a battery on top.

"Ava beat Emily at four squares. Emily cried," Mike announced, not to be outdone.

Irene nodded, taking the car from Dave. "Wow, that must have been exciting. A new four squares champion." Mike nodded excitedly. "Dave, this is so cool. Does it work?" He nodded and took it back. "We'll test it out later." Irene stepped inside, putting her bag on the couch.

Angie and Jason didn't move far from the door, clearly anxious to be off. "We got pizza," Angie told her. "Put it in the oven when you're ready. There's salad in the fridge."

Irene nodded. "When do you guys expect to be back?"

Angie looked evasive. "Oh, after the kids are in bed."

Irene gave her a long look. "Angie, please. Tomorrow is a field day for me. I want to get home."

"Why don't you stay in the guest room? Then you don't have to worry about it."

"That wasn't our deal. I want to get home so I can take off fresh in the morning."

Angie looked at the bag. "Didn't you bring a change of clothes?"

Irene sighed. "I did but not work clothes."

Angie frowned. "Why didn't you bring work clothes?"

"Because," Irene said, with strained patience, "you

told me that you wouldn't be late."

"We won't be," Angie said too quickly. "We both have to work tomorrow. We'll have a few drinks, dance, then take a cab home."

"And what time would that be?" Irene said impatiently.

"Eleven?"

Irene glared. If Angie said eleven, it would be closer to midnight.

"No." She picked up her bag. "I'm going home. Find another babysitter."

"Fine. We'll be back here by ten," Angie grumbled.

"Nine."

"I feel like I'm on curfew, Mom," Angie mocked.

"Next time, why don't you call Jennifer?" Irene said sweetly.

Jason, who had been listening to the conversation, finally contributed. "Hey, don't worry, Irene. We could all use some more beauty sleep. We'll be home in time for you to get some."

"Thank you, Jason," Irene said.

After Jason and Angie left, Irene and the boys planned their evening. They decided to make their pizza and eat before going out. Though she offered to take them to a new neighborhood for geocaching, Mike and Dave opted for the splash pad at the park instead. The three of them took the bicycles to Memorial Park, and after a tour of the perimeter, Irene settled down to watch the boys run, leap, and twirl through the water.

They returned to the house by seven thirty, and Irene set the three of them up with rounds of video games. Of course, she quickly lost, leaving Mike and Dave to maneuver their characters around the various challenges.

As it was a school night, the boys were soon being herded up to brush their teeth, get in their pajamas, and get to bed. Irene read an extra story or two, and by eight-thirty, both were asleep in their bunks.

Irene sat down at the kitchen table and pulled out her laptop, hoping to catch up on email. While she was waiting for it to boot up, she called Sharon to check on Percy.

An hour later, Irene acknowledged that she was done. Her eyes weren't going to focus on another email. She packed up her various personal items and placed the bag by the door. She took out a book and decided to read on the couch until Jason and Angie arrived. Within ten minutes, she was asleep.

Sometime after midnight she was startled awake by the door opening. Jason and Angie lurched into the house, loudly admonishing each other to be quiet. Irene stretched, checked her watch, and scowled at the pair of them. She could see both had been drinking and knew that any further discussion would be futile; it couldn't be more obvious the pair was anxious to head upstairs. Angie was making feeble excuses, but even those were diminished by Jason's joking instance that "Irene understood" and they should "go upstairs, baby."

Without saying a word, Irene got up, grabbed her bag, and headed to her car. She didn't slam the door, but only because she didn't want to wake the boys.

"Gosh, she's really steamed," she heard Jason announce through the door, followed by drunken giggles.

Chapter 14

Including her nap on the couch, Irene got six hours of sleep that night. Thursday morning, she and Peter drove back to Lakelynn. The lack of sleep dragged on her, but as Peter drove and she inhaled coffee, they discussed the most recent events.

"What did the auditor tell you?" Irene asked.

"He's not happy. They're always late on the closing of the books, but they capture everything. There are some significant gaps in separation of duties that we'll cover." He paused. "And it took them a while to catch this, but someone has been tampering with the banking records."

Irene's brow lifted. "Tampering? How?"

"As you know, there are hundreds of checks marked ruined." Peter tapped the brake, almost making Irene spill her coffee. "They told us it was because they were putting them in the printer the wrong way. But, for every check run, there is always one or two screwy checks."

"Screwy?" Irene repeated.

"The checks go through the bank. They cover legitimate expenses, matched to an invoice. But the checks don't match what is recorded in the system."

Making Irene nervous, he reached into the back seat to pull out a three-ring binder. He handed it to her. "Flip to the tab."

She did and studied the notes. The banking

statement showed check 1002 was never cashed. But in the ledger check 1002 paid an invoice to a well-known office supply company. The bank recorded check 1018 as paying the expense.

Irene studied the pages. "Where are the missing checks?"

"Sometimes the check is never recorded," Peter said, clearly excited. "Sometimes it's been used to pay something we can track back to an invoice. Sometimes it's something else."

Irene noticed his speed and winced. "Slow down, please. Why can't you look at the banking statements to see who it was made out to?"

"Because," Peter said in an ominous tone, "on the records they've been using to reconcile the bank statements, these checks have been altered to look like they were made out to a legitimate vendor, referencing a non-existent invoice."

"So, the bank statement is correct, but no one is seeing these checks go through the system."

"Yes."

Irene thought about this for a moment. "Do you have a list of checks?"

"Flip to the next page," Peter directed.

She did.

"We have not been able to link any of those," he murmured as he deftly moved through early morning traffic.

"Can you go into the bank system and look up the information?"

"Yes, that would be the logical next step," he said. "Here's the fun part."

Irene took a deep breath and waited.

"Betty Hacher has been receiving statements through the mail every month. The address looks absolutely legitimate. But when we called the bank, we learned that no one currently working at the city has a log-in."

Irene blinked. "*No one*?"

Peter nodded.

"Let me get this straight. The city manager doesn't have a log-in."

He nodded again.

"Or the finance director."

Another nod.

"The mayor? Board chair? Harvey the Rabbit?"

"We didn't ask about Harvey," Peter said, deadpan.

"I find it hard to believe that Betty Hacher has been okay with all this."

Peter shrugged. "I don't know if she's fine or not, but when I asked her to pursue it, she told me that if they ask for more records, it will cost money."

Irene was quiet for several miles, thinking about this information. Wearily, she outlined the next steps. "I'll call John and ask him to get the ball rolling on a warrant. After that, I'll talk to Rusty and see what we can do about the bank." She returned the binder to the back seat. "Where does this leave the audit?"

"The auditors will complete field work by Friday," Peter reported. "They may have to come back a few times, but they've made good progress." He shrugged. "Of course, until they get the answers about these checks, they can't finish anything."

"Right."

****

They arrived at the city hall by nine a.m. and

delivered coffee to share with the audit team.

To prepare for the day's work, Irene had researched the timing of various employee resignations to verify the causes of the city's overall chaos. As advertised, many of the upper management in the general administration departments left after Lynda Sherry was sworn in as mayor.

Irene had also reviewed the mayor's biographical data. A Navy brat, Lynda landed in Oregon after her own career in the Navy ended. Interestingly, she had left the Navy with a general discharge under honorable conditions; not an honorable discharge, Irene noted. While she often touted her military service, the details of why she left the service were not discussed on record. Irene searched for mention of where the mayor had been stationed and her rank, and discovered Lynda entered the Navy as an enlisted member and worked as a yeoman her entire six-year career at Everett Naval Station. It was unusual for any six-year stint in the armed forces to not result in at least one promotion.

After the Navy, Lynda had worked at a plastics factory in eastern Oregon, as a hostess in Idaho, and as a manager at a convenience store. Then, in an abrupt change, she had moved to Lakelynn and got a lower-level management position at the local paper mill. From there, she had started to appear as a local pundit on the municipal scene, talking her way into the center of the local political party. She had taken great pains to paint herself as a hard-luck story made good. Furthermore, she used her background as leverage for her skepticism of the government and its spending. Irene found several interviews where she painted local officials in the worst possible light, turning ordinary regulatory matters into a grand conspiracy.

The one thing Irene did not find was any accounting experience or management titles. She was not convinced Lynda knew enough to pull any kind of accounting scheme.

Irene and Peter planned to spend the day interviewing the remaining city finance staff. Interviews were an important part of any audit process, but there was no standard list of questions. They would focus on separation of duties and any recent changes that might point to wrongdoing.

The first interview was with Andrew Fergus.

"Andrew, can you describe your position for us?" Irene began.

Andrew, who looked to be in his mid-twenties, took an audible swallow, his Adam's apple bobbing in spite of his round face. "Well, I do the basic AP entry. Account payable," he clarified quickly.

"Do you see payroll or grants?" Peter asked.

"No. Just the bills."

"How do the bills get to you?" Irene asked.

Andrew shifted a nervous gaze to her. "They are in a box on my desk."

"Who puts them there?" she asked.

"Everyone. The receptionist brings over bills from the other departments and puts them in my box. But sometimes the department heads bring one over, particularly if it's something they need quickly."

"How do you know the payments are authorized?" Irene inquired. "Does someone cross check the bills to invoices or contracts? Who signs off on the expense?"

"The department heads fill out a sheet about how to code the bills and then sign the sheet."

"How do you know who is signing?"

"Mostly, it's easy. You see the same thing every month. But sometimes I have to call over and get a verification."

"What happens to prompt you to do that?"

"Oh, when the numbers don't add up. Or when they don't use a correct account code. Or if I don't recognize a signature. Lots of reasons, but those are the main ones."

"Do you think it's a good system?" Peter asked.

Andrew looked confused. "Well, you know, it's the one we use."

"Do many mistakes come through?" Irene asked.

"Well—" He gulped nervously. "—they aren't careful about using the correct account codes. And sometimes they don't sign things, so it has to go back to them."

"Do they get mad when that happens?" Irene asked.

Irene could see the young man's desire to be helpful war with his need not to get anyone in trouble. Finally, he said, "There are a couple of managers who lose patience quickly."

Irene nodded. "That's common."

Andrew nodded gratefully. "Yeah. I try not to take it personally. I mean," he chattered, "I know the department folks have more important things than coding their office supplies correctly. I get it. I mean, they have work to do. But I'm doing my job, too, when I ask about what code they mean."

"So, they're not using the correct codes?"

"Sometimes they write 'federal education' grant; sometimes they don't use the codes at all. And I try, but we have several codes from the education department. I don't know which one they mean. If I don't use the right code, the billing and reimbursement doesn't work out," he said earnestly. "The gal in accounts receivable showed me how hard it is to figure out expenses if you use the wrong code."

"How did she do that?" Irene asked gently.

"We had to reconcile an account at the end of last year. She was doing a final bill, and the grant was overspent in personnel and in supplies. We had to go back through everything and re-sort the expenses, and then we had to ask for a budget amendment. We ended up having to give back some money because we weren't allowed to spend money on some of the things."

Neither Irene or Peter asked which grant it was. Both had heard versions of this story in other audits; it was so common as to be unremarkable.

"What do you think could be improved in the system?" Peter asked.

Andrew paused before saying, "I do wish they were more respectful. You know, do it right the first time. Their attitude is like it's my job to fix things. But I think it's more their job to get it right from the beginning."

Irene nodded. "Program managers don't understand how important money is until they run out."

Andrew nodded.

Peter pulled out an invoice he had selected. "Did you pay this invoice?"

Andrew took it and frowned. "Well, I don't pay the invoices. I mean, I don't cut checks. I just enter them into the system. But I don't think I entered this one."

"Why not?"

"I always enter my initials down under the 'entered' stamp. It's the way I was taught, and I always try to remember. There was a problem a couple of years ago with an invoice, and no one could figure out who entered it."

Peter made a note. "Why isn't this one initialed?"

Andrew took the paper again. "I don't know. That's kind of weird. The only other person who enters invoices is Kathy Nicols, the assistant director. Or maybe Betty Hacher, but I've never seen that."

"When would Kathy or Betty enter an invoice?" Irene asked.

"They don't. They are the ones who cut the checks. They shouldn't be doing this end." He shrugged. "I guess I forgot to initial it. It came from the public works department, though. Sometimes they need a fast turnaround."

Irene nodded. "And you know that because of the code?"

Andrew nodded. "It's for the sidewalk bond."

Irene made a note. "The sidewalk bond?"

"About four years ago the city passed a bond to redo the sidewalks in the worst part of town. The money is almost gone, but we still get a few invoices every now and then."

"After you enter invoices, what's the next step?" Peter asked, moving on.

"I prepare a list of transactions for Kathy. She reviews and signs off on them."

"So, she reviews everything," Peter summarized, making a note.

Andrew looked to the ceiling as if he was pondering the statement. "I think she looks at the bottom line and account numbers more than the individual checks. Like, one time she made me take off a whole stack of bills and hold them for two weeks because we didn't have some money in yet." His voice held an edge of excited titillation. "Another time, she wouldn't let me pay a whole set of bills until the grant manager did a review."

"Can you tell us more about that?" Irene asked.

Andrew shook his head, looking genuinely regretful. "I'm not sure what Kathy told him, but the grant manager came storming over and they had a big argument. Betty came in later and all three of them were arguing."

"How do you know that?"

"My cubicle is right outside Kathy's office," Andrew said, his eyes bright. "I couldn't help but overhear."

"When did this happen?" Irene asked, making her own notes.

"Last month."

"If checks are held back, for whatever reason, how is that recorded?" Peter asked.

Andrew looked confused. "What do you mean?"

"Is a note put into the file about the delayed payment?" Irene stepped in. "Does a memo go in a file?"

Andrew thought for a moment. "We file all the invoices by vendor, so I'm not sure we'd keep anything about when a particular item was paid or if there was a delay."

Irene had a thought. "Can you check to see who entered it in the system?"

Andrew shook his head. "Sorry, no. The system doesn't record the user information." He studied the invoice a litter longer. "I don't recognize this signature." He handed it back. "A mystery, I guess."

"A mystery," Irene agreed.

Chapter 15

Next, Irene and Peter met with Anne Kiley, who entered accounts receivable. As both Irene and Peter knew, her job was to make sure that grants, taxes, and other revenue streams are identified and sorted correctly. Personal and property taxes were collected at the county level, which was cited as a reason for having only one AR position.

Irene and Peter asked Anne to describe the AR process. Who was involved? Who marked items pending? "The city gets an electric funds transfer notice when the funds come through, but you don't necessarily see what account the money should go into?" Irene asked.

"That's right," Anne replied. "Usually, I'm able to match the EFTs against the known invoices. If I can't, I call the bank; they give us more information."

"Do you check property tax income against your own list of properties?" Irene asked.

"No. We get an inventory from Clackamas County," Anne said with a shrug. She was a pretty, non-descript woman in her fifties. Irene had the strong impression Anne had no trouble leaving her job behind at the office.

"How do you know if a new property development has been added to the tax roll?" Irene pressed.

Anne looked blank. "I don't know. I guess the county does all that."

"Do you work with records to compile lists of recent building activity?"

Anne paused. "Well, I sure don't. Betty might know more about that."

Irene made a careful note. "Betty is the one who checks property tax income?"

Anne nodded. "She's the one who generates the invoices for those income streams. I work with the regular monthly stuff. Betty does the irregular stuff. She tells me where to book it, and I do. I know certain kinds of taxes go in certain accounts, but Betty sorts out what is put into what account."

"How many accounts are there?" Peter asked.

"We have four bank accounts, but there are lots of funds within those accounts, such as the library fund, the fire fund, all those different funds."

Peter nodded. "And Betty is the one who decided how much money to code into each fund."

Again, Anne nodded. "Each fund gets a certain percentage of the money."

"Who decides what percentage?" Irene asked.

"Betty. I mean, I guess she talked with Rusty or someone."

"Do you know where Betty stores the allocation schedule?"

Anne took a sip of her drink. Irene noted it was a frothy pink concoction from across the road. "We have spreadsheets that are updated all the time."

"But not necessarily paper files?" Peter clarified.

Anne looked confused. "Sure. We have files of the deposits and stuff and how we divide everything."

"If there is a change from the budget, how is that documented?"

"I don't know. Betty must do it. She's in charge of the spreadsheet."

After Anne left, Irene studied Peter. "What are you thinking?"

"I overheard the audit staff comment that income is being distributed differently than what the formal budget outlines."

Irene nodded. Making sure revenue streams were properly categorized was important. If one program was getting more money than they should, it stood to reason another program was receiving less. Additionally, revenue streams could be diverted; if the city was receiving one hundred dollars but only recording ninety-nine of that, the other dollar was going somewhere.

****

Irene and Peter took advantage of a fifteen-minute break between interviews and walked over to the coffee shop.

"There are two things that bother me," Irene broke in after they sat in a quiet corner of the café and would not be overheard. "The check situation is one, obviously. But there is something off with the revenue situation. Why are they out of money for a public works program? What did the auditors spot about revenue allocation? Based on what I've heard, they are using everything they have to cover holes. Had someone told you about the argument between Betty and Kathy a few months ago?"

"What's the story?" Peter asked.

Irene took a sip of coffee. "The city received a new grant for storm water treatment. It appears they did the contracting in a proper manner and even got some of it done. Then Kathy Nicols told them they had to stop because the money was gone."

Peter shrugged. "I take it that was unexpected?"

"Very," Irene said dryly. "I've only heard bits and pieces. No one involved has been forthcoming. But piecing things together, the revenue was recorded to general funds, not to a special grant code."

"Oh, boy."

"They were careful about billing the expenses to the correct fund code, but there wasn't enough revenue to cover the expenses. When they figured out the problem, instead of fixing the revenue, they did a journal entry to move all the grant expenses into general funds."

Peter nodded, listening intently.

"Under normal circumstances, that would be enough to earn a finding. Possibly, even pursue fraud charges," Irene reasoned. "They must have figured that out, because a month later, they moved the expenses and revenue back into the grant account."

"It could be just a fix," Peter said doubtfully.

Irene took a bite of her croissant and chewed thoroughly. "Possible. Betty was on vacation during the initial discovery. And she's the one who moved the revenue and expenses back into the grant fund. But when I reviewed the spreadsheet summing everything up, the calculations were wrong. Around seven percent of the revenue was left in the general fund."

Peter nodded. "Interesting."

"Indeed."

****

On paper, Rose Davis was more than qualified to run the payroll process. With more than twenty-five years of experience working in payroll, she may have even been overqualified. Most people with that level of experience choose to move up in the hierarchy.

Before Irene and Peter even began to ask their first question, Rose said, "I grew up here in Lakelynn and have lived here all my life. And before you ask, I haven't moved up any higher because I didn't want to. I don't want to be in management and deal with all those politicians. I like my job; I like going home and not thinking about my job."

Irene smiled. "I understand that. Is there anything that would make your job better?"

"The same stuff that's been going on since God invented forms. People don't turn in their time sheets on time. They don't get them approved. They move. They have babies. They decide they want to become penguin caretakers and leave. People are the thorns."

Irene couldn't help it. She smiled and looked down at her legal pad.

Peter was obviously amused as well. "Anything except people problems?"

Rose rolled her eyes with dramatic humor. "Don't get me started on the time sheet audits. You'd think they'd have it down by now."

"But they don't."

Rose made a motion mimicking writing. "Of course not. You practically have to hold their hands to get them to enter what they are doing."

"How often do you do audits?" Peter asked.

"We do them every quarter, like the procedure says," she responded briskly. "And before you ask, yes, we need to get better about squaring up the actuals against the books."

"You don't do that?"

"I would," Rose responded, drawing out the word to suggest exasperation. "But Betty insists I send over an

Excel sheet of the changes, so I do. Every three months. Like clockwork. And then—" She gasped in mock horror. "—they didn't get entered."

Irene smiled again. "Why not?"

Rose dropped the sarcasm. "She will get around to it, but she's slow. I beg her to let me do the spreadsheets monthly, so we can square up billing with the various grants. But she won't do it. So, that means there's a delay on closing."

"Why do you think she's insisting on doing it herself?" Peter asked, making notes.

"She's concerned about separation of duties. Specifically, she doesn't want to give people access to the accounts and the ability to make journal entries."

"How would you go about improving the process?"

"I'd give more people clearance to make journal entries but give fewer people the power to approve them. Our software allows that, but right now only Betty and Kathy do the journal entries." She paused. "Or, I should say, the software upgrade we paid for last year would allow that, but it hasn't been installed."

Peter looked up from his legal pad. "Why not?"

Rose's face went blank. "You'll have to ask Betty."

"Walk us through the current payroll system," Peter invited, dropping the subject.

"Everyone is issued a paper timesheet. They fill it out over the course of the month, then give it to their supervisor. The supervisor signs off, then gives it to me. Then I make the entries into the system. As I said before, we do a quarterly audit to adjust federal funds to match the timesheets."

"Do you get pressure to pay people who don't have timesheets?"

"Of course," Rose said swiftly, then took a deep breath. "To be fair, it's not that simple. If someone is entered in the system, the system will generate a paycheck whether there is a timesheet or not. If there are any changes, they are reflected in the next month's pay. But technically, we're not supposed to pay anyone without having that timesheet. And, of course, we do. So many people do direct deposit that it would be a nightmare to actually hold back people's paychecks."

"But do you get pressure to look the other way?"

Rose nodded. "Most of the supervisors know that I never 'look the other way' and that I never give up. My title should be nagger-in-chief."

Peter smiled. "Does anyone else sign off on the payroll run?"

"Betty looks at the overall amount, but I don't think she looks at the personnel list."

"Do you ever see changes that need to be made?"

"All the time," she said easily. "That's why I could use more lead time."

"What do you do if you see a change or a mistake?"

"It has to go back to the supervisor."

"You don't ever adjust it yourself?" Peter asked.

"Can't do it. If I changed one, everyone would want theirs changed when they made a mistake."

"But you could?" Petter pressed.

"I could," she admitted. "But I don't."

Peter was busy writing, so Irene asked, "Does Betty ever check the procedure? Check to make sure it's going the way it should? That your formulas are correct?"

Rose paused. Irene could see her weighing her response. Once again, her face went blank before she said, "No."

"Who wrote the current operating procedure?" Irene asked curiously.

"The last finance director."

"Did he check it?"

Rose nodded. "He insisted everyone's desk manual was up to date, and if you changed something, you changed that. He was great about making sure no one was cutting corners on procedure. Once a year, he'd require everyone to go over their desk manual."

"And Betty?"

"She has a different management style than Mark."

Irene nodded and thought for a moment. "Fair enough. From the standpoint of this audit and helping us understand how things are supposed to work versus how they actually work, what do you think are the biggest holes in the system?"

Rose eyed her warily, but apparently decided Irene wasn't going to make her talk specifically about Betty. "The department is chronically understaffed. Because of that, we're always behind. There is almost no way to have an effective set of checks and balances because everyone is always trying to keep their head about the water."

Irene met Rose's eyes. "How many positions do you think need to be added?"

"I could use an assistant. And another person for both accounts payable and account receivable. That would give everyone a chance to do quality checks."

"And?" Irene nudged.

But Rose shook her head.

Irene studied Rose. "Tell me if I'm wrong?" She waited for Rose to nod her head. "Betty is a good finance professional, but not much of a manager. She tends to think short term instead of long term." Rose didn't say anything. "Why do you think Betty is the finance manager?

Rose held Irene's gaze for a long moment. Finally, she sighed. "Theoretically, if I agreed with that assessment, and I haven't said I do, I would say she is here because nature abhors a vacuum."

Irene tilted her head.

"We had some good managers. Then the mayor got elected and started pushing her whole 'fiscal experiment' agenda." Rose ran her tongue around her lips in a nervous gesture. "I don't care what anyone tells you, those managers didn't retire or find another job or whatever. They left. And Betty stepped into that vacuum. She was assistant director. I guess it made sense to appoint her."

"And then?" Irene asked.

Rose seemed to debate her response for several moments before she continued, "Betty isn't my favorite person, but she also isn't a bad person. She doesn't have the chops to be finance director. But possibly worse, she doesn't have the political knowledge to insulate her staff from what's going on here, so finance has lost close to fifty percent of the staff. Most of the other departments are operating at a quarter loss, but we've been hit hard here because there is no one to get in the way."

Irene nodded. "Thank you for explaining that theory." She paused, then said. "Out of curiosity, would you take the director position if they offered it to you?"

"No," Rose responded without hesitation. "When I go home, I'm done. And I want it to stay that way."

Chapter 16

Irene and Peter stacked interviews like blocks. They were on a tight schedule with five interviews before lunch and three after. Irene wanted to leave by late afternoon so she could make it to her agility class by half-past six. While they waited, Irene scanned Kathy Nicols's resumé and employment timeline.

Kathy had come on board the city of Lakelynn as a fiscal analyst six years ago. When Betty accepted the management position, Kathy had applied for the assistant position. With a bachelor's degree in finance, she'd worked in Nevada and Arizona before moving to Oregon. With fifteen years of accounting and finance experience, Irene thought she was probably biding her time, waiting for the right position to move up.

Irene had spoken to her several times on her first day in Lakelynn, but since then, their interactions had been mainly the exchange of emails. Her initial impression was of a contained, competent individual. Someone willing to wait and see rather than fight. Cool and watchful. Her name had come up in many procedures, and Irene had speculated that she held responsibility without power. Like Betty, Kathy had access to every part of the financial process. Unlike Betty, Kathy stayed under the radar.

Kathy arrived promptly at the given time. Again, she was dressed in a long floral-print dress and demure flats.

Her hair was pulled back in a barrette. Irene noticed she was again worrying her wedding ring. Peter greeted her warmly, as she had been helpful during this process. He settled her down with an offer of a drink. Irene could tell he had come to respect Kathy.

"What a day." Peter began, inviting Kathy to laugh with him.

Kathy twisted her wedding ring. "It's crazy," she said quietly.

Peter nodded. "Audits can be intense, even without all the…big personalities."

Kathy shot a submissive look at Irene. "And you're saying there has been some embezzlement; I don't want to end up accusing anyone."

"Let's start out easy," Irene murmured. "We'd mostly like to talk about bill payments. Someone told me you wouldn't authorize payment on some bills. Tell me about that."

Kathy licked her lips. "What do you mean?"

Irene checked her notes. "About four months ago some stormwater bills came in from public works." She took some bills out of a folder and laid them on the table to jog her memory. "I was told that you delayed payment on them. Can you tell us why?"

Kathy looked through the copies. "I think I remember this. They had offered a contract without authorization from finance. There was no more money allocated to that program."

Irene returned the bills to the folder. "When we looked over the files, money had been drawn down to cover the expenses. More than enough because there haven't been many expenses to cover."

"That's not the way we do things," Kathy stated.

"How do you *do things*?" Peter asked.

"We code the expenses to the accounts, then do a monthly drawdown for necessary funds. For grants like this, we prefer to work on a reimbursement basis. We can draw down more frequently, depending on the grant." She thought about it for a moment. "Maybe Betty did."

She shrugged. "But the reason I didn't want to approve the payment was because was the contract had never been put in the system. There was no budget authority to purchase the items. It wasn't an approved expense."

"Even though the program manager signed off on the expenses?" Irene asked, pointed to a signature on the invoice.

Kathy began to look flustered. "If the contract doesn't go through the system, there is nothing to provide the information on the vendor and coding. You have to look up the contract number in order to set the bill against it. For those bills, when I looked at the balance on the account, other contracts had already appropriated all the funds. There was no money left for the contract, which would have been discovered if it went through the process."

"What ended up happening?" Irene asked.

Kathy paused for a moment. "I know the contract got paid. Rusty came down and authorized it all. He told me to code it to the storm-water grant, even though we didn't have enough to cover it, so I paid it. That's the last I heard about it."

Irene was making notes on her legal pad and didn't meet Kathy's eyes. "Did you ever talk to Betty about it?"

"I did. She told me some older contracts had been paid on that account, but they shouldn't have been. No one had caught it, so we had to make some journal entries to fix it."

"Why had they already drawn all the grant?"

Kathy shrugged. "Same reason, I guess. Revenue isn't my part. Betty works with accounts receivable to keep things in balance."

"Tell us about the approval process on accounts payable," Peter requested.

Kathy looked doubtful. "Surely, you've heard about it from everyone else. And we've given you the procedure."

Peter smiled. "We tend to want to go over the same processes."

She gave a small, impatient sigh. "The program managers have a form where they provide an account code and signature, authorizing the transaction. It can be a bit of a struggle to get everyone to fill in everything correctly."

Peter asked, "And then?"

"It gets routed to finance. Usually, one of the receptionists brings it by. And it gets entered into the system. About once a week, I'll prepare a check run."

Irene cut in to ask her own question. "How do you know who enters what?"

"We don't worry about it. There's an Entered stamp which we all use when we're done. That's all that's necessary."

Irene pulled out a copy of one of the Willamette Falls Consulting invoices. "So, you don't know who entered this."

Kathy took the paper gingerly. "Is this one of the ones that got embezzled?"

"We don't know. That's what we're trying to figure

out."

She looked it over, front and back. "There's no way to tell who entered it."

"It doesn't show in the computer? No one initials their entry?"

"No. It's never been a problem."

Irene nodded. "What about the authorization? Can you tell me anything about who authorized the payment?"

Kathy examined the paper again. "I don't recognize the signature, but the code is for public works. I'm not sure what department. I'd have to look it up." She glanced up. "Do you want me to check for you?"

"You can get me a code list after we're done. Nothing else strikes you about the authorization or the check?"

"Sorry, nothing."

Irene let Peter asked a few more questions about the process before moving in the direction of management. "I've heard stories about how the mayor has been interfering with the finance process. What's your take on that?"

Kathy looked hesitant. "I don't want to talk about the mayor. I don't think it's my place to criticize her."

Irene nodded. "Politicians make policy, not interfere in the day to day running of things."

Kathy looked down at her hands, twisting her wedding ring.

"Okay," Irene said. "Let's take this from another angle. How often would you say she comes into the fiscal offices?"

Kathy raised her head. "Oh, we usually see her a few times a week. And I know that Betty meets with her and

Rusty once a week."

"That's not too unusual," Peter said in a soothing tone.

"Maybe not," she said, but didn't look convinced.

"What kinds of things does she ask for?" Irene asked. "The mayor, I mean."

Kathy frowned. "It's not like she's asking for specific things, directly. But she's always fluttering around, saying we should 'tighten the belt' and telling everyone not to make unnecessary purchases. Which isn't bad, but she's so fierce about it, you hate to buy anything. Betty told me the mayor actually looks over purchases of office supplies."

"What happens if she thinks something isn't warranted?" Irene asked.

"She'll explode. I mean, it's literally worth your job."

"She can't fire you," Irene pointed out. "Why is your job at risk?"

"She might not be able to fire you, but she'll tell the managers to do it. Or give you bad reviews. I had a friend over at the library, said that they had a clerk who put in an order for magazine holders, and when the mayor saw it, she told the library director to fire the clerk or she'd take out the budget lines for two clerks next year. I don't know if the director did or didn't, but my friends says that they have been told to cut the new book budget by fifty percent the last three months, no matter what it says in the budget."

Both Irene and Peter made notes.

"Interesting," said Peter. "Tell be about the budgeting process."

"That's Betty's thing. I run some numbers and

reports, but Betty runs the budgets."

"How do you distribute revenue to the various departments?"

"I don't know. Betty has never let me do that part of the process."

Sensing a dead end, Irene moved to the next question. "Why have there been so many destroyed checks in the last couple of years?"

Kathy looked resigned. "We've been over this before."

Peter smiled. "Like I said, we often go over the same stuff multiple times."

In a pedantic tone, Kathy recited, "We got a new printer-copier and did a couple of runs wrong. We made a sign, but someone thought the sign was wrong and changed it. We changed it back, but then the sign went missing, and no one had saved the digital version, so we had to go through the whole process again.

"We finally got it sorted out. Then we noticed the number of checks run was *huge*. We eventually found out someone was entering expenses and marking them so every expense was printed on its own check, instead of consolidating payments."

Peter nodded sympathetically. "There haven't been as many problems lately, but there have still been some destroyed checks."

"Yes. It's impossible to not have the occasional check become unnecessary or get held up."

"Industry standard is about one percent," Irene commented. "That's one out of every hundred checks. Lakelynn was running at twenty percent last year and seven percent this year."

Kathy looked startled. "I guess I didn't realize it was

that high. Is that a problem?"

"I'm surprised," Irene continued, "so many people want a check. Most companies are asking for direct deposit or electronic funds transfer."

Kathy shrugged. "Some of the vendors want it. The contractors tend to like it because they can match checks to invoices. We haven't pushed direct deposit because that involves banking fees. It isn't much less expensive than cutting a check."

"Do you know of any staff members who specifically want a check instead of direct deposit?"

Kathy shook her head.

"What kind of process do you guys have before you cut a check for a new entity?" Irene inquired.

"We get a W-9 or I-9, of course," Kathy answered quickly.

Irene nodded. "We followed up on a handful of contractors and couldn't find a W-9 on file. Why do you think that would be?"

Kathy shrugged again. "If we started using them several years ago, the W-9 has probably been filed in some other year."

Both Irene and Peter made notes.

Peter picked up the questioning next. "Who normally has access to the check stock?"

"We keep it locked in a drawer. Both Betty and I have a key. So does Rusty."

"Where is the drawer?"

Kathy sighed. "In the filing cabinet with the personnel records. Several managers have access to that, but there's a second key needed to open the drawer with the check stock."

"And you're sure no one else has the second key

except you, Betty, and Rusty?" Peter pressed.

"They shouldn't. In six years, I haven't seen another person get into that drawer."

"But you haven't always had access to the check stock," Irene asked. "You were only promoted to your position six months ago."

Kathy nodded. "But I did the check runs even before that."

Irene nodded. "Is the system the same now? Do you give the checks to someone else? Or do you still take the checks to the printer yourself?"

Kathy paused for a moment. "I never thought about it. I guess I give them to someone else if we're busy. But I usually try to keep an eye on the stock."

"Do you inventory the checks when you take them out of the drawer? Or when you give them to someone else?"

"No. It's never been an issue. I'm right there. I can see the printer from my desk." She looked at Peter. "I've never heard of having controls on the check stock, other than locking it up."

Peter nodded. "It is frequently overlooked." He looked at Irene and she gave a small nod. "I think that's the end of the questions we have for you. I can't promise we won't ask more, but I think you can take off. Thanks for your patience."

She nodded, looking relieved. "Okay. I'll see you later."

Chapter 17

Betty Hacher arrived on time for her appointment, again with a mile-wide chip on her shoulder. Once again, Irene was struck by the inappropriateness of the jeans and wide-strapped tank top. Irene didn't have a problem with a simple wardrobe, but it was easy to imagine her at a backyard barbeque. Irene tried to visualize her as a decisive professional, leading the city's finances and failed.

"Thanks for coming, Betty," Peter started.

"Like I had a choice," she snapped.

Peter gave the smallest of sighs. "Well, we appreciate your time, no matter what."

She snorted. "I smell a witch hunt."

Peter paused and gave her a steady look. "Nothing has been finalized yet."

She scoffed. "I know you'll bury us in findings. I think you should modify—"

"I can't discuss my report with you," Peter said firmly. "We've been hired by the board and our report belongs to them."

After she flopped back in her chair with a sulky look on her face, Irene studied her. "I'm surprised you're giving Peter such a hard time about this," she said coolly. "With you being a CPA, I would have thought you'd understand the process."

Betty straightened. "I understand the process. But

that doesn't mean—"

Irene cut her off. "Stop interfering in the audit."

Attacked rather than the attacker, Betty lashed out. "Don't you tell me what to do. It's my job."

Irene scoffed. "If you knew how to do your job, none of us would be here. The audits would have been done on time, and we wouldn't be chasing an embezzler." She paused. "But I guess you didn't worry about that."

Betty's face went beet red. "I've done nothing but worry about that. I've told Rusty and Lynda we need more staff."

"I don't think—" Irene turned away from Betty to speak directly to Peter. "—we should continue talking to her. She's obviously a suspect and only interested in covering her tracks."

Peter looked startled at Irene's brash tone. "I'm not sure we're *there*, Irene."

Irene shook her head. "You could have fooled me. Look at the revenue allocation." She tossed the report on the table between them. "Why would she be allocating funds like that unless she was trying to conceal revenue for her own purposes?"

"I'm not concealing revenue," Betty bellowed.

Irene turned back to her. "Oh? Then why have you distributed less than half the general funds budget in public works, schools, and safety to the actual programs?" She picked up the report and tossed it to Betty. "It's all there. All those programs are in the red, but the general fund is sitting pretty. That might not be so bad, except you've run up the lines of credit to get more cash and billed out every grant you could get your hands on. The programs are under budget on spending, but you are still asking for more cuts because you say the money isn't there."

"That's the way we do cash flow," Betty snarled.

"Since when?" Irene asked. "I've looked at the books for the last ten years, and this year is the first time you've chunked out revenue differently than the budget plan."

Betty's face set into a hard line. "You don't know anything about cash flow."

Irene turned away from her again. "Peter, go to the other revenues. We'll deal with her when we're ready to file charges."

"You don't know anything about it." Betty growled. "We're trying to maximize our interest revenue. It's good cash management."

Irene gave her an incredulous look. "Since when?"

"It's something Lynda and I have been working on this year."

"So, you and the mayor have cooked up a scheme where you're dumping money into the general fund and leaving all the other funds overdrawn." Irene met Peter's eyes. "Sure. That's great cash management."

"You don't know that it won't work," Betty raged. "This could be the answer to government overspending."

"How?" Peter asked quietly while Irene made an incredulous noise and pulled out her phone as if to check text messages.

Betty snapped, "If we make all the departments think they don't have any extra money, they won't spend it on anything that's not essential."

While Betty shot defiant looks at Irene, Peter said gently, "The flaw in your logic, Betty, is that the council doesn't just give spending authority. They provide a detailed plan about how money should be allocated in order to meet that spending plan."

"There is leeway in that system," Betty shot back. "The council doesn't care as long as we can pay our bills. They don't want to hear about the day-to-day worries of having enough cash on hand."

Irene looked up from her phone to mutter, "Well, you've done a great job of making sure they don't have to get educated on *that* issue."

Peter caught her eye, giving her a quizzical look. When she didn't respond, he continued. "You'll have to adjust things at the end of the year. What was your plan for taking care of that?"

Betty looked down at her hands for a brief moment before meeting Peter's gaze again. "It's no big deal. We'll do a journal entry."

"Something of that size," Peter started doubtfully, "would require approval. And you run the risk of the council deciding to spend this chunk of money they have lying around."

Betty shook her head vehemently. "No. That wouldn't have happened." She stopped and made a visible effort to reword the thought. "Lynda and I have talked about this. She won't let them do that."

Irene put down her phone and leaned forward in her chair. "Lynda won't let the council spend the money. Lynda will help you do this big journal entry. Lynda has this big idea to improve cash flow." She paused. "And you aren't worried about being the scapegoat when it all goes wrong." Betty's eyes shifted away from Irene's. "Like it is right now, Betty? Where is Lynda now?"

"You just don't like her," Betty said sullenly.

"Fair enough," Irene admitted. "But unlike you,"

she paused meaningfully, "I don't have to like someone to do my job."

And with that, Irene picked up her briefcase and left the room.

****

Twenty minutes later, Peter came into their working conference room, shutting the door solidly behind him. "What was all that?"

"I was doing good cop, bad cop. I should have let you know it was coming," Irene said, her tone apologetic. "She doesn't get it. I thought it was time to shake her up."

He rolled his eyes. "Mission accomplished. So, did you get anything out of that other than to make her spitting mad?"

Irene smiled. "Making her mad was my goal. She's not going to break unless we put some real pressure on her, and we can't do that as long as we're letting her dictate the shots by complaining all the time."

"She called you some names, went on about her thirty years of experience. She thinks you look down on her because she let her CPA drop. But nothing new or interesting."

"Did you know about the revenue adjustments?" Irene asked.

Peter shook his head. "Nope. It must be something new this year, and we haven't been looking at that. We've been focusing on the past due audits."

Irene nodded. "Yes, it's new. I can't figure out why Betty is going along with it. She should know better."

Peter shrugged. "I'm going to be glad when this audit is over."

Chapter 18

Irene and Peter interviewed the city council members after lunch. First on the list was Robert Austin. Robert was a successful family law attorney who had dabbled in politics for years, though before this stint he had mostly been involved in city planning committees that got into papers and other media-savvy events.

Irene had gleaned that he was not heavily engaged in the process of managing the city. He was more interested in media exposure and meeting important people. Peter had reviewed his council attendance and told her he didn't do the work but never missed the party. An online search turned up many articles with his name, primarily showing him smiling in front of a courthouse.

Irene needed Robert to fill in a few blanks. She didn't consider him a suspect; he was utterly unconcerned about accounting and did not have access to the check stock. Still, there were a couple of details that made her wonder if there was more going on than met the eye.

After she and Peter were settled, Peter took Robert through the basics of the audit process. "So, Mr. Austin," he began, "the city council has the responsibility for authorizing expenditures. You approve the budget and delegate authority to the various department heads to get things done. Tell us how you yourself fit into that process."

Robert nodded. "Well, it's a basically a rubber stamp process. The staff tells us what we should do, and we approve it. I mean, obviously we try to get money for things that are important to us, or we campaigned on. We might try to cut some things we don't think are important. But mostly, it's agreeing with what the city manager puts in front of us."

"How far in advance do you see the budget?"

"Oh, I don't know. We're always looking at one budget or another. I know there's a big meeting in January." He smiled conspiratorially. "I think I missed it this year."

Peter didn't bat an eyelash. "Jayne Tanaka serves as the budget chair. How much influence does she have in the process? As opposed to the other council members? Or the mayor?"

Robert looked bemused. "I'm not sure. Jayne has always kept the process under tight constraints. I know this year Lynda worked on it because Jayne had to be away so much."

"Committee notes say that you stepped in for Ms. Tanaka as the budget chair last year."

"No." He looked startled. "No, that can't be right."

Peter pushed the published minutes toward him. "It says that you were the budget chair."

Robert leaned back to look at the ceiling, then said, "Well, yes, it may *say* that, but Lynda did all the work. I'm far too busy to deal with that kind of thing."

"So, you lied?" Peter asked coolly.

"No. No." Robert shook his head vehemently. "I was the chairperson in name only. I presented the budget, but Lynda did all the work. She handed it to me at the last minute." He shifted his gaze to Irene. "You know how it is."

"How was it?" Irene asked smoothly. "Did you review it before you presented at the public meeting?"

He shrugged. "No. Everything balanced, so what would have been the point?"

"So, no one other than you and Lynda saw the budget before it was presented at the public city council meeting," Irene clarified. "Not the city manager because there wasn't one at that time. Not the previous budget chair; she was taking care of her husband. Not even the head of finance."

"Well...yes." The penny was starting to drop.

"So, no one accept the mayor looked at the numbers."

Robert turned on the charm that probably served him well in court. "It's true that I wasn't as involved in the budget process as I should have been. But it doesn't follow that the budget was flawed." His sharp, affable smile was clearly meant to invite understanding.

"Of course not," Peter said briskly. "I'm not suggesting that. I'm trying to establish the budget process." He paused for a long moment. "And why, after the budget was adopted, the city's revenues have not been allocated according to that budget schedule."

"What do you mean?"

Peter handed Robert a piece of paper. "This is an analysis of the approved budget revenues versus cash to date. In the next column, it shows where the cash has been placed." Again, he waited a moment while Robert studied the paper. "In case it's not obvious, it looks like the city has extra general fund money, but the individual programs have received all but nothing."

Robert looked baffled. "So?"

"So," Peter said, drawing out the word, "the net result is that it looks like the mayor has kept her campaign promise. The city has more money in the bank. Costs have gone down because every program is cash strapped. And now there is extra money. That kind of thing makes a good campaign platform, right?"

Robert stared at Peter, then shifted his gaze to Irene.

"I don't understand what your young man is getting at."

Irene raised an eyebrow. "I would have thought that was obvious. As assistant investigator at the Oregon Office of Adjudication, Peter is asking if you were aware of a plan to manipulate city revenues to enhance your political position."

Robert looked back and forth between them. "A plan? It's accounting. Aren't there supposed to be all those checks and balances?"

"The mayor has done a good job getting those out of the way. The finance department is massively understaffed. There's almost no one who understands where the money should go. And the people who do are in no position to stand up to the mayor."

"There wasn't a…plan," Robert said, his voice tapering off.

Irene waited. "There wasn't a plan. Okay." She looked down at her notes. "Did you, as the chair of the budget committee, review the monthly budget versus actual reports?"

He was beginning to look alarmed. "Was I supposed to?"

"It's part of the chair's job. They make a report to the city council and the council approves the report."

"I'm sure we do that," Robert blustered. "At every

meeting there's something about budget approval."

"But do you review it?"

Robert said nothing. It was obvious that his lawyer instincts were starting to kick in and he was reluctant to continue. Irene and Peter let the silence drag out.

After a full minute, Peter said, "Mr. Austin, the audit will tell the story. We'll relay any—" He paused for emphasis. "—oversights to the audit team to put into the report."

Robert turned his eyes to Irene.

She responded to the unspoken question. "The OA is concerned with breaking the law. Bad judgment is not a crime. This doesn't mean we won't charge you with a crime if we find out that you've committed one, but our scope is narrow."

He nodded and looked down at his hands for a minute. "I don't think I've broken any laws. But it's becoming clear that I have exercised bad judgment." He blew out a deep breath. "I'm not good with all the fiscal stuff. I took over the budget committee because Jayne was struggling. As mayor, Lynda can't officially present it, but she told me she could help."

"How did she help?" Peter asked.

"Basically, she did it for me. She passed me the presentation a couple days before the meeting." Again, he looked at one of them, then the other, searching for absolution. "I don't have time to do more than the bare minimum."

"Did you get the sense that Lynda had an agenda?"

"Lynda always has an agenda," Robert said bitterly. "But I didn't think that cutting a few corners and cleaning out a few desks would create this kind of problem. Basically, Lynda's right. Governments spend too much. I don't agree with her on all of the particulars. I didn't even vote for her. But she's got the best interests of the taxpayers at heart."

Peter nodded. "So, it's fair to say that you rubber-stamped the budget process and the monthly reports. You didn't review them or ask anyone about them."

Robert nodded glumly.

Chapter 19

Peter and Irene pushed Robert hard but were unable to uncover more than a general indolence toward the duties of his position. This was a sharp contrast to city councilor Bill Henley who appeared tired and worn, as if he carried the weight of the world on his shoulders.

"So, Mr. Henley, it's my understanding that this is your first year in office," Peter began.

Bill nodded.

Peter hesitated a moment before continuing. "You may not have been through an audit before, so let me tell you about what we are looking for. The city council has the responsibility for authorizing expenditures. You approve the budget and delegate authority to the various department heads to get things done. I'm interested in how you fit into that process and if you have noticed anything unusual about it."

Bill nodded; it was a few moments before he spoke. "I want to start out by saying that I've been doing volunteer work for twenty years. I thought, now that I was retired, that I could serve the city by being a council member. I've followed politics for years. I've been on the library board and the school board. But being on the council has been harder than I ever thought it could be. And this? This had been a shock. I'm not sure I can handle it."

Peter nodded. "It can be hard," he said

sympathetically. "What's been the hardest?"

Again, Bill paused to think. "The vitriol. No one," he shook his head. "No one has anything except the city's best interests at heart. Yet people treat you like you're the enemy."

"You were elected at the same time as Mayor Sherry," Peter clarified.

"Yes. Jayne told me that it's been worse this round because she has stirred people up so much. But I'm not sure I believe it."

"That's made it difficult to do your job?"

"Yes. Every time I look at a report, I wonder if I'm going to get hate mail if I agree—or more hate mail if I disagree. When the budget comes up, I can't even look at the reports. All I can think about are the people who marched through town on Tax Day."

Peter looked at his notes. "There was a riot?"

"I'm not sure we officially called it a riot, but people tipped over a police car and busted out a few windows at City Hall. They sprayed graffiti. Someone even fired a gun at the front door. The police had to use tear gas to disperse the crowds." His eyes met Irene's. "And then there are all these 'alt' groups. You can't please anyone. No one wants to compromise. And if you compromise, they call you a traitor."

"Public life is a harsh reality," said Irene sympathetically. "I know I'd never run for office."

Bill nodded. "I don't want to be here. I've decided to resign."

Irene nodded. "I understand. But if I can offer some advice, get through the audit before you make a decision. Many things are happening and it's important not to overreact."

Bill sighed heavily. "Maybe."

Peter took up the reins of the interview again. "How did you work with the other council members on getting the new budget approved?"

****

Jayne Tanaka was the final interview of the day, and Irene was glad. The late night, paired with the drama and emotions of the day's interviews, made her glad Peter would be the designated driver for the trip back to Salem.

Jayne wore a well-fitting pleated dress in a bold peacock blue paired with tasteful gold accessories. The look was not so formal that it would have drawn undue notice, but it was clear that she had chosen her wardrobe with care. Irene found Jayne Tanaka an interesting and admirable woman. She was a history professor at Portland State University and had lived in the Portland area all her life, moving to Lakelynn in 1982. According to her website, she had been involved in local political activism since her children were in school. She had been on the city council for over seven years, and her website announced she would not be running for reelection when her term ended next year.

After settling in their chairs, Peter guided Jayne along the now familiar line of questioning. "Ms. Tanaka, the city council has the responsibility for authorizing expenditures. You approve the budget and delegate authority to the various department heads to get things done. Tell us how you fit into that process."

"Until last year, I had been the budget chair for five years."

"Why did you step down?"

"My husband had a stroke. That led to the discovery that he had developed pancreatic cancer."

"I'm sorry to hear that."

She nodded. "He had the stroke right after Thanksgiving and was diagnosed in December. He died in March."

"That must have been hard."

"Yes. And I'm afraid I didn't handle it well. Or, more accurately, I didn't handle anything else well. I should have stepped down from the council."

"Why didn't you step down?"

"I tried. I turned in my resignation letter. But Lynda came to me and said that they could handle things for a few months until we got past the worst of it. I know it wasn't proper, but she told me no one needed to know. That they'd keep things moving until I could come back."

"And you believed her?"

Jayne looked down at her folded hands. "I don't like Lynda. I actively campaigned against her. After she was elected, she went out of her way to let me know there were no hard feelings. But I still didn't like her."

She sighed. "I always felt guilty about that. I hate that so much of politics is binary, and I believe in working together. But it's hard when there are more people like her running for office. People who don't know the first thing about government. I'm a history professor. I believe in the adage 'those who do not know their history are doomed to repeat it.' It breaks my heart to see people like Lynda elected."

She swallowed visibly and took a sip of water from her water bottle. "Because of that, I feared I was being too hard on her. She's the antithesis of everything I believe in. But I told myself she couldn't be as bad as I believed."

Jayne smiled faintly. "Charlie told me I needed to look for the good in her." She took another sip of water and visibly struggled for control. Irene and Peter waited patiently. "When Charlie was diagnosed, I don't think I believed it for a while. I thought if I could take care of him, he'd make it. Then he died. I tried to go on with life." She shook her head.

"A friend talked me into going to a grief support group. After a few months, I started to come out of the haze. When I looked around, I realized Joseph, the old city manager, was gone. I realized that Lynda had the reins. And it snapped me back."

She squared her shoulders and sat up a straighter in her chair. "I pushed to get a new city manager in place, but the hiring process bogged down." She sighed. "I see now that Lynda was behind that. I was still struggling personally and couldn't handle much. I thought about resigning again, but I was scared to leave things the way they were. We finally managed to get Rusty on board, and I hoped that he would be able to get control of the situation." She shook her head. "I don't know if that was even possible."

When she was sure Jayne was done speaking, Irene made a subtle gesture to Peter that she would take over the interview. "Jayne, first of all, I'm sorry for your loss. I truly commend you for struggling through a difficult time and doing your best to serve the people of Lakelynn."

Jayne nodded, dabbing at her eyes.

"Peter and I aren't here to make things more difficult. We're here to help you and the other council members address a difficult situation." She paused, making sure Jayne was engaged again. "To that end, it would help if we put our chips on the table." Another pause. "What, exactly, was 'the situation' as you understood it?"

Jayne licked her lips. "I knew we were behind on the audits. That was an issue. I knew the new school building wasn't going well. It dragged everything down. Then there were the personnel problems. We lost several upper-level managers when Lynda came on."

"Why do you think they left?" Irene asked, wanting to clarify the issue.

Jayne rolled her eyes. "The city manager he had worked for the city for more than twenty years. I don't think he was planning to retire, but the day after the election, he put in his notice. I asked him to stay on for three months to get us through the transition, and he did, but not a minute longer."

"Were their conflicts between him and Lynda?" Irene asked.

Jayne smiled. "He was too professional to get into hysterical screaming matches. It was clear he didn't like her. He laid out a course of action, and that was it. Lynda felt like she could override him, and he didn't agree."

Irene nodded. "And the finance director left."

Jayne laughed mirthlessly. "He didn't even find an excuse. He told me that he was going to find another job. 'And if she wins, I'll give my notice the next day.' And that's what he did."

"How did Betty get hired?"

Jayne sighed. "I told Lynda we shouldn't hire her for the position, but she was available."

"Why did you think she wasn't a good fit?"

Jayne compressed her mouth in a way that indicated she wasn't sure about having to say more. "The former finance manager wasn't happy with her performance. She made a good lower-level employee. High maintenance, but good. The trouble began when she accepted a promotion. It quickly became apparent she couldn't supervise or make decisions. The finance manager mentioned it to the city manager, and he told me. Based on that, I told Lynda she doesn't have a managerial temperament, makes questionable decisions."

"What did he question?"

"He wasn't sure if she understood when someone had crossed the line. She let some questionable purchases go through, even though the relationship between the contractor and the staff personnel was close. I know there was one instance where she allowed someone to hire their father-in-law."

Irene made a note. "Do you know the contractor's name? Or the staff member?"

Jayne shook her head.

"Why didn't you ask for her removal?"

"I wasn't up to much. Charlie had started to have problems, and I was much missing in action. I mentioned it once to Bill. I don't know if he did anything."

"Why do you think that was?"

"I'm not sure," Jayne admitted. "Maybe the sheer conflict got to him. Lynda is such a strong presence. So divisive. At first, he didn't hesitate to speak up when he disagreed with her. Then the mail started coming in. Honestly, I've never seen anything like it. We usually get some comments, or the paper writes an editorial. Something about Lynda brings them out of the woodwork. Every council meeting ended with angry constituents, and our phones would ring for days afterward. It was more like a circus than a city council meeting."

"And you think that got to him?"

"It got to me, and I work with college kids. Bill was a doctor. I think he was used to difficult people, but not public life." She sighed wearily. "What sane person is?"

Chapter 20

After the interview with Jayne Tanaka, Irene and Peter stopped for the day. Peter drove them back to the Salem office. Though rush hour traffic increased their travel time, they were still able to clock out for the day just after five, which allowed Irene to change clothes, eat dinner, and load up Percy in time to get to dog agility class. They arrived at the barn a few minutes early. A nearby field, provided for handlers to exercise their dogs, allowed her to give Percy a quick walk.

Irene took classes from Kate Affeson, a local trainer. Kate had set up class in the inside arena. This left an exterior arena available for use as a grassy practice area. The grass wasn't perfectly flat because moles and other critters had created little rises or hollows. The equipment was older and heavier, but still functional. The area was perfect to provide younger dogs a new exciting place to practice various exercises.

When time permitted, Irene liked to spend a few minutes playing with Percy in the little space. Tonight, his eyes were bright at the thought of agility and his tail was waving merrily. He gave a soft whine. Irene looked at the course and saw some easy tunnel/jump discrimination challenges had been set up.

"Okay."

Percy darted out toward the equipment, spun, shook, gave a sharp bark of excitement, and waited for her to toss the rope.

"Tunnel."

Percy took off toward the chute, and when he came out, Irene threw his rope. He dashed after it and shook it dead, then brought it back hopefully. Irene took it, then moved into position beside the jumps. Percy was a quick dog, and to handle him well, her movements had to match and direct his. As she was working a back cross to get him to change direction, she noticed her left foot was tingling. She ignored it and continued playing with Percy for a few minutes.

Ten minutes later, she set up Percy back in the car. He greedily slurped up the water in his dish before settling down to pant happily in his crate. The car was in the shade, but she still opened all windows and back hatch, then draped a shade cloth over the car. She turned on the portable fans which sat above five-gallon buckets of water to create a cooling mist. Finally, she topped off Percy's water and set out his cool mat. In the ninety-degree heat, Irene wished she could be as comfortably housed. She picked up her chair and entered the training barn.

It was noisy, as usual. The dogs, of course, were not the ones making the noise. Friends chatted, handlers shouted orders at their dogs, and Kate bellowed instructions at the handlers. More misting fans were stationed throughout the area, serving the dual purpose of keeping things cooler and settling the dust.

Sharon was sitting next to the handler of the darling young Basenji whom she'd seen at the recent agility trial. Irene sat in her chair and leaned over the x-pen to give the puppy a pat. "How's this young man doing?"

His handler puffed up with pride. "He's picking it

up. He'd rather play with the other dogs and people, but he's just a baby."

Irene laughed. "Yes. The brain software doesn't install for a few years."

Another handler entered the barn and set up her chair next to Irene. After the group greeted her, they asked about her young Australian Sheepdog.

"Full of it as usual. I wish I could give him more exercise, but I have to work and sleep too."

They all laughed.

"How did the trial go last weekend?" Irene asked.

She smiled proudly. "Two Q's and a first place. Percy looked good on Saturday, but I don't think we saw you on Sunday?"

Irene nodded. "He was entered, but after the first run, we bowed out. That trial's so hot, and Percy's getting older." She turned back to Jamie's handler. "How did Jamie do at the breed show?"

"He got a major. Two more points and he's finished." They all looked down at Jamie, who sat on the mat, looking pleased with himself.

"He's such a cutie."

"I'm telling you, get a Basenji for your next dog. Stop fooling around with those Aussies."

"Never!" Sharon promised.

They laughed together. Kate gave a few words finishing words to the class, then said, "Next class. Come out and let's talk."

Irene and seven others walked out to the center of the ring to listen to Kate.

Kate had bought the land and half-built barn years ago when the previous owner had abruptly lost interest in her horse hobby and had decided to sell her half-finished, state-of-the-art equine playground. Over the years, Kate had converted the facility to dog training and boarding, resulting in a well-kept, well-lighted, pleasant, modern training space. It was outside of town near forest land with no nearby neighbors to complain about the barking dogs.

Kate made her living with dogs, through a combination of boarding, training, and doggie day care. She was a consciousness instructor and innovative trainer; her generosity blanketed her students, dog sports in general, and agility in particular. She allowed local agility club members to rent barn time to work on the practices she had set up or devise their own challenges. "So, those of you who trialed last weekend could have used more front crosses, but most of you either didn't use it or bungled it." She gave a handler named Liz a stern look. Liz blushed. "So, I set up a couple of opportunities to practice here."

While Kate outlined the course challenges, Irene began to wonder if participating in the class when she was so tried was a good move. A small voice in the back of her head, sounding like Dr. Mandeville and Sharon, told her to take it easy. She told herself she was worrying too much and continued with the lesson. A few minutes before her turn, she returned to the car and uncrated Percy. He stretched and wagged his tail before prancing off to sniff the smells. Within a few moments, they were entering the barn to wait their turn.

The course was set up with a series of jumps in a hashtag shape. The trick was to guide the dog over the necessary jumps before moving into a sequence of contact obstacles or tunnels. Per her plan, Irene asked Percy to stay at the start line and moved forward to give herself a head start. When she released him, he launched himself with enthusiasm, and they were off. Handling the first set of obstacles went off without a problem, with Irene and Percy performing a front cross flawlessly. Percy rocketed out of a tunnel faster than Irene expected, and she felt slow guiding him through the second course correction. As he went over the second jump, Irene tripped and reflexively threw out both arms. She hit the ground shoulder first. Out of the corner of her eye she saw Percy try to change direction. He caught the jump cup with the inside of his leg, yelped, and hit the ground.

Irene scrambled up from the dirt and ran over to him. Kate had already rushed to him and was holding him quiet. He stood, holding up his right back leg, a large gash visible on his inner leg dripped blood. He looked up at Irene with big worried, trusting eyes.

"Okay, let's go."

Irene reached town and tried to pick up her fifty-pound dog. Her body ached from the fall, and she dimly recognized that her left shoulder wasn't working properly. Her mind lagged from shock and exhaustion. Dimly, she heard the other class members crooning at Percy and asking if everything was okay. Irene felt like crying.

She felt like yelling, "Of course everything is not okay. My dog is hurt." Instead, she admitted, "I can't carry him to the car. Can someone help me?"

Several people offered, and within minutes, Percy was in the car, and they were headed for the emergency vet. Once there, he was taken in the back to be sewn up. Irene waited, cursing herself. Thirty minutes later, the vet came out to tell her that Percy had only needed a couple of stitches and he'd be able to come home that evening. He gave Irene some painkillers for the dog and told her to keep him quiet for a couple of days.

Once at home, Irene pulled out a heated dog bed and draped some towels over it in case Percy needed the warmth. He ignored the offering and lay on the cool kitchen tile in the heat of the late summer evening.

She sank onto one of her barstools. Waves of emotion swamped her. This wasn't going to be okay. No amount of denial was going to enable her to continue her life as it was. Why hadn't she considered that Percy could be hurt as a result of her stubbornness? Why hadn't she said no to babysitting the night before? Or not come to class when she realized she was tired?

She couldn't trust her body. She had MS.

Now that the adrenaline ebbed, she began to notice how badly her shoulder hurt. She tried to lift her left arm but cried out from the almost excruciating pain. Taking deep breaths, she tried to decide on a course of action. Surely, she was sore from the fall and emotionally strung out. She went to the bathroom, took some pain killers followed by a warm shower, then tried to fall asleep. She lay awake, her mind spinning, her body aching.

Around one in the morning, she got out of bed to sit in the living room chair after carefully applying ice to the areas that felt the worst. By three a.m., she admitted that she would have to go to urgent care first thing in the morning. Her arm and shoulder were stiff and swollen. She was unable to move the entire left side of her body.

Irene didn't want to drive herself to urgent care. She debated the merits of getting a ride share to the doctor's office versus asking Sharon or her sister. By eight, she was dressed and had messaged her boss that she needed a sick day. Putting her coffee in a travel mug, she awkwardly carried the beverage onto the front porch. Percy followed her. He wasn't limping but moved with slow care that hinted at soreness. Irene thought they looked like they were auditioning for a geriatric product commercial.

Her phone pinged moments later with a message from Sharon asking how she was. Drained, she texted back that she was okay, knowing her response would do nothing to reassure Sharon and would only serve to let her know she was awake. Sure enough, she saw Sharon's curtain flicker and knew her friend would be coming over to join her within moments. Irene accepted that Sharon would take her to the doctor. Percy came over and put his head in her lap, looking up with worried brown eyes. She caressed the top of his head.

Sure enough, within minutes, Sharon was cutting across their tiny front yards to join her on the porch. Percy saw her and wagged his tail as hard as he could. Sharon stopped to talk to him and give him a cuddle. Percy rolled onto his back, giving her the perfect opportunity to check his stitches.

"Looking good," Sharon murmured, giving his tummy a thump. She looked up at Irene. "Unlike you."

"Thanks."

Sharon studied her intently. "What's wrong?"

Irene didn't even try to hide her problem. "I hurt my arm and shoulder in the fall yesterday. Would you be able to take me to urgent care this morning?"

Sharon frowned. "Hurt? How?"

Irene couldn't help herself. She snapped, "I fought gravity and gravity won. It's called a fall."

Sharon gave her a stern look. "Why didn't you mention this last night?"

She approached Irene and made as if to examine her shoulder. Irene pulled back. "Don't. It hurts."

Hands still extended, Sharon said. "Maybe it's something I can fix for you?" She did several kinds of body work as part of running Hands to Soul Healing Center.

"I need to see a doctor," Irene said, teeth gritted.

Sharon took a step back. "Okay." She decided not to push. "Let me change my shoes and I'll be ready to go."

Chapter 21

Hours later, Irene was more than ready to head home. Her left arm was in a sling after being diagnosed with a rotator cuff injury to her shoulder and her wrist and elbow with a good sprain. She was to report back to her regular doctor in two weeks to rule out the possibility of a tendon tear.

She was fully dressed, but waiting for the printed after-care instructions when the exam door opened, and Dr. Mandeville came in. "Hello, Irene."

Dr. Mandy Mandeville was a neurologist and the last of the long line of doctors Irene had been to in the last six months to get a diagnosis for the muscle spasticity and balance problems. In her mid-forties, she gave off an air of impatient competence that Irene found perversely reassuring. She was small, dark haired, and dressed in a lab coat over clothes that looked like they had come straight from the local thrift store.

"So, I see you took my advice about taking it easy," Dr. Mandeville said, surveying Irene's sling with a baleful look.

Irene remained silent.

Dr. Mandeville sighed. "You can't beat this. It's not about willpower. But if you make some simple changes, we can control it. The sooner you address this, the better your long-term chances."

Irene averted her eyes.

"Have you taken any time off? Did you talk to your boss about taking a lighter workload?"

"It's been busy," Irene admitted. "The office is short staffed. And I got a new case." Her voice was as calm and reasonable as she could make it.

Dr. Mandeville scowled. "Seriously? Do I need to check you into the hospital to get you to take care of yourself?"

"I won't go," Irene said stubbornly.

"It would give you an excuse to take some time off."

"I have the sick leave, but I have too much to do."

Clearly struggling for patience, Mandeville sat down in the chair across from Irene. "Your body is attacking your nerves. It could stop tomorrow, and you could go into remission for years. But it's more likely that this attack will get worse until you make some changes."

Impatient with herself and everything in general, Irene snapped, "You're being an extremist. Attacks can have symptoms from mild to severe. This injury doesn't have anything to with MS."

"Doesn't it?"

"I tripped."

"Muscle coordination and spasms are symptoms, as well as vision problems."

"I *tripped*." Irene repeated.

"Fine. Keep doing what you're doing. And you'll end up in a wheelchair."

The thought of a wheelchair made Irene's chest tighten. She looked away.

"What about support?" Mandeville continued. "You haven't told your boss or co-workers. Have you told your family? Your friends?"

"I'm not ready to tell my family. I told my friend, Sharon."

"Irene, you need to take time off and deal with this. The tests aren't final, but you and I both know that you have MS."

Sharon walked in and overheard the last words. "Irene, it's MS? For sure? You said the tests weren't looking good."

"I see I was optimistic, thinking you had told your friend," Dr. Mandeville commented dryly.

"I don't need this!" Irene burst out. "I just really do not. It's my life and my body and I'll do this in my own freaking way." Irene rose from the examination table. "Sharon, I'm ready to go."

Sharon studied Irene doubtfully. "Not to interrupt this grand display, but have you actually finished the doctor's visit?" She turned to Dr. Mandeville and extended her hand. "I'm Sharon, Irene's chauffeur, apparently."

The nurse reentered the room, sheaf of papers in hand. Irene snatched them. "Now I'm done."

Dr. Mandeville rolled her eyes. "Nice to meet you, Sharon. I'm Dr. Mandeville and I've been attempting to advise Irene."

"Got a hammer?" Sharon quipped. Mandeville laughed. Irene glared at both of them.

"Okay," Sharon said soothingly. "I'll take you home."

Irene closed her eyes, struggling for control. "I have to stop at the pharmacy first."

Sharon smirked, catching Mandeville's eye again. "Of course."

Irene glared at the pair of them.

****

Sharon placed a cup of tea on the little table next to Irene's favorite chair. "Drink some tea."

She reached for a throw, but Irene pushed it aside crankily. "It's going to be ninety."

Patiently, Sharon told her, "Take a nap. I'm going to go get your prescriptions, then I'll fix some dinner for when you're hungry."

"My insurance card and cash are in my bag. I don't understand why we couldn't have stopped on the way home."

"Because you are tired and in pain."

"You don't have to take care of me," Irene growled.

Sharon replied sweetly, "I know. I want to. And because you make it *so* much fun."

After swallowing feelings of anger and rebellion, Irene took a deep breath. "I just need to be alone for a while. I'll take that nap."

"You know, we're not trying to make you do anything. We're worried about you."

"I'm fine."

"Yes, I'm familiar with your motto. Tell me when the engraved plaque arrives."

In response, Irene set her jaw. "I'll deal with it in my own way."

"You can't keep going along like nothing has changed."

Irene studied Sharon's earnest face. She didn't know how to stop the conversation, and she couldn't explain her feelings. She searched for a way to bring the discussion to a close. "I hear what you are saying. I am going to take it easy. But right now, I don't want to talk about this anymore. I'm tired. I hurt. And I just want to sit for a while."

Sharon looked like she wanted to argue but finally nodded. "Okay. I'll get the prescriptions. But I am making you dinner."

"Thank you."

An hour later Irene had dinner in the fridge, painkillers next to her tea, her dog with her, and the house blissfully empty of people.

She woke up in the mid-afternoon, sore and emotionally exhausted. She got up and padded gingerly down the hall to the bathroom, then to the kitchen to pour herself a large glass of iced tea. Percy followed, supervising her every move. She let him into the backyard and did a few gentle arm stretches while she waited for him. Restless, she thought about her afternoon.

Irene rarely had free time, even on the weekends. She didn't take extended weekends to compete in distant locations, but there were enough local trials that she and Percy competed every couple of months. When there wasn't a trial, she went to classes, workshops, and practices. Of course, there was all the usual housework to keep on top of, and she spent as much time with her nephews as she could manage. Add church, family lunches, friends, and the flotsam of daily life, and she was lucky to get an hour or two to read.

It was unusual for her to be at home in the middle of the day with nothing to do. She read for an hour but couldn't shake the restlessness. With a guilty look at Sharon's house, Irene got out her laptop. She'd check some emails, maybe catch up on some reports. She quickly discovered that typing aggravated her shoulder, so she scanned for items to read.

Within moments, her mind started to drift as though now that she was trying to do something productive, her brain decided to process the events of the last twenty-four hours. She closed down the report she was reading and scrolled to a bookmarked internet site.

But like the other times she had looked, there wasn't a cure for MS listed.

Irene had Multiple Sclerosis, an autoimmune disease that causes the body to attack its own nerve cells. The possible symptom list was extensive and daunting.

Currently, her symptoms were limited to dizziness, fatigue, and loss of muscle control which included spasticity, numbness, and tremors. Dr. Mandeville assured her that her case was mild and that with some basic care, she had every chance of going into remission. Remission basically meant there would be no degeneration until the next attack, which could come at any time.

As she had told Sharon, the diagnosis wasn't one hundred percent yet. One of the many appointments and tests she had over the next few weeks could pick up a different diagnosis. Irene wasn't fooling herself. Dr. Mandeville had made it clear that her lifestyle would have to change. That what she considered normal was now over.

MS seemed to affect people with high stress lifestyles, her job as a state fraud investigator certainly qualified.

MS could cause cognitive problems, such as difficulty concentrating or remembering information; her job demanded attention to detail, research, and lightning-fast recall.

MS could lead to extreme mobility problems; her

favorite hobby was dog agility.

She reread the site. And began to cry.

She was hurt.

She was scared.

She was overwhelmed.

Chapter 22

Irene took it easy on Saturday. On Sunday morning, when her alarm went off at six like it did every day, she took a quick inventory and decided more painkillers would be a high priority, though her overall pain level was improving. Percy took no kind of inventory; he began trying to herd her downstairs to get his food. She got up and shuffled to feed him. Ten seconds later he was fed, and she let him into the backyard.

In spite of being tired, she hadn't slept well. Again. Though the medication dulled everything, the pain was still raw enough to prevent the escape into sleep. Irene took a shower to loosen up, then dressed in yoga pants and a soft sweatshirt and took Percy to the dog park at Minto Brown so he could get some real exercise. He liked to play with other dogs and usually could find a playmate for his favorite games.

At the park, she quickly spotted some of Percy's regular playmates and turned him loose, then gingerly walked to a park bench to sip her coffee. Periodically, Percy would check in, but he was happy to be there. When a few dogs went home, he trotted back, and Irene threw his ball for a while.

After slurping up a drink from his portable bowl, Percy decided to relax in the shade. He was panting happily when Irene's phone rang. She saw the caller ID but chose to answer anyway. "This is Irene."

"Are you coming to church today?" Jennifer demanded.

Irene thought about it. "I don't think so. I'm not feeling great."

Jennifer scoffed. "Don't make excuses. I'm taking Angie and her family out after church. I want you to join us. I'm meeting a client at three, so I don't have time to come see you."

Irene simply rolled both eyes and sighed. She was never *invited* to lunch but told to *tag along* with Angie's family. She had hoped to avoid Jennifer, but she needed to talk to Angie about babysitting the boys.

"All right. I'll see you there."

About an hour later, dressed in a loose cotton dress and flats, Irene walked into the medium-sized neighborhood church. Her arm was in a sling, but she had made sure any bruises were covered.

Jennifer was waiting by the front door, serving in her usual position as greeter. She graciously welcomed the families to church, displaying her amazing memory for names and asking after various personal details. Her warm smile made every churchgoer feel special. When Irene moved up the line to present herself to her mother, Jennifer didn't waste her megawatt smile on her but shifted her gaze to the groups behind her.

"Why weren't you earlier?" she asked crossly. "I wanted you to help me unload the treats."

"I'm sorry. I'm moving slow today."

Jennifer looked at her sling, and for the first time her expression shifted. "Well, go make sure there's enough coffee. Make another pot if you think we need it."

"Sure." *And with that she was dismissed.*

Irene moved to the kitchen and checked the

industrial coffee pots sitting on the kitchen pass-through that adjoined the vestibule. The church had an open coffee policy before church; after services, the teen group operated an espresso machine and sold baked goods to raise money.

Irene exchanged greetings with one of the older kitchen workers. She wondered why her mother thought she needed to check the pot. She fended off questions about her sling, explaining she had taken a hard fall and needed support until she healed. Irene discussed the coffee levels with another woman and agreed that another pot of coffee wouldn't be a bad thing.

A few minutes later, Irene made her way to the nave and took a seat near the back. She chose the seat because it was near a family with children. When Jennifer entered, she scowled at Irene and made her way to a front pew with no children. Irene smiled down at the nearby little girl who was earnestly coloring in her book.

Irene was never sure if Jennifer was actually religious or if she looked at church as the most readily available method of getting clients, but she attended church services nearly every Sunday. She was also active in several popular, non-religious local clubs and charities, almost certainly for the same reason. In Jennifer's defense, she put energy into these enterprises.

After services, Jennifer caught up with Irene. "Why did you sit in the back? You know I like to sit in the front. There was room and I laid out my coat to save you a seat."

"I'm sorry. I didn't see it," Irene responded truthfully.

Jennifer studied her again. Normally expressionless to prevent possible wrinkles, she risked a small frown.

"You said you had an accident. What happened?"

"I had a fall. Nothing important. What time are we meeting Angie?"

"Noon." Suspicion had finally gripped Jennifer, which came out in the form of an accusation. "You look pale. Why didn't you put on makeup?"

"Because I almost never wear makeup."

Jennifer pursed her lips. "You'd attract more attention if you spent more time on your appearance. You always dress so plainly. People will think you're a lesbian."

Irene had heard this before. "I'll keep that in mind." She looked at her watch. "The sermon went long. Where are we meeting Angie? We don't want to be late."

Jennifer waved her hand. "Marco Polo. It will only take a few minutes to get there."

Irene was saved from further interrogation when a robust older couple came up to her to ask Jennifer about the possibility of downsizing.

Irene went to get a latte, then hurried to one of the plush chairs near the entrance. She took out her water bottle, then opened a biscotti she had purchased that morning. She took a deep breath and told herself to relax.

As a child, she'd been scared of her mother. While Jennifer could be charming, she tended to save it for clients—past, present, or future. She was a goal-oriented woman who didn't suffer fools, which had not translated to a warm, motherly relationship with either of her children.

After Irene's father was killed in a Navy accident when she was eighteen months old, Jennifer threw herself into making sure they were financially secure. Attractive, organized, and a skilled negotiator; within a year she was one of the top realtors in the area. They had money and stability, but she had been too busy and often too tired for warmth.

When Jennifer met her second husband, Mathew Rane, five years later, Irene remembered a brief period of warmth. There had been family outings to parks or the children's museum, movie nights, and board games. Then Angie was born and crying, and whispered conversations replaced the quiet family times. The fights had started, and by the time Angie was three, Jennifer was again on her own.

Whether it was a result of the divorce or Jennifer's natural competitive nature, being a top realtor was no longer enough. She had to be the best realtor in town and pursued that goal to the near exclusion of any other consideration.

Irene had always felt fortunate that Jennifer's fixation on her career slowed her ability to date. Two marriages and a few boyfriends appeared to be enough for Jennifer. Irene was entering high school when Brian Neilsen had convinced Jennifer to come to his agency, and eventually to become his wife.

Brian was twenty years older than Jennifer, but he was smooth, charming, and warm. Angie had become fond of him, and the marriage had appeared to be a strong one through Irene high school and college years. Even the first few years into her accounting career, Jennifer had been content.

Then the housing bubble burst.

By that time, Brian and Jennifer owned the brokerage together. Jennifer was still actively selling real estate, and they should have been able to stay afloat with some downsizing. But Brian had forgotten to tell her that he had taken some chances in the housing market, putting money into developments that were now unable to continue. The debt soon drained away every ounce of their combined safety net.

To her credit, Jennifer had stood by her man. Right up until the day he died of a heart attack.

With Irene starting her career and Angie a few months away from high school graduation, Jennifer could have sold or closed the business and continued as a realtor until the housing market rebounded. It would have been lean, but possible. Instead, Jennifer took every ounce of determination she had honed through the years and ruthlessly kept her business afloat and on top. Angie's decision to elope with Jason had interfered with Jennifer's focus for a few weeks, but in the end, she had kept her business and reputation.

Irene reminded herself that her childhood had not been difficult. She and Angie had never wanted for anything physically. But Jennifer's time, attention, and approval had been the price paid for the material possessions. Irene was blessed with an independent attitude that didn't make her crave Jennifer's approval, but Angie still longed for Jennifer to become a doting grandmother.

Angie often claimed that Irene saw Jennifer's faults too clearly. Irene preferred to think of it as realism. When she had purchased her home, taking advantage of the burst housing bubble, Jennifer hadn't even pretended to try to steer her toward a good value. She had wanted Irene to buy the biggest house she could afford, preferably from Jennifer's inventory. When Irene had insisted on buying a small older home near the state buildings, Jennifer had barely spoken to her for weeks after the deal had closed. She had messengered over her standard realtor's gift basket for a house-warming present.

Twenty minutes later, Jennifer approached Irene's chair. "Are you ready for lunch?"

Irene had thought about excusing herself, but she was starting to loosen up and thought she might as well get the explanations over with. "Sure. I'll be okay."

Jennifer nodded stiffly. "I'd offer you a ride, but I have to do a showing after."

"No worries."

Irene left church and made her way to Marco Polo, a local restaurant that offered Asian, Chinese, and Italian, with varieties to please vegans and gluten-free diners. She arrived first, and asked the server for appetizers, drinks, and crayons for the boys. She also asked the waiter to bring out plates so the group could share dishes and asked for three of the boys' favorite dishes to be served about ten minutes after everyone arrived. If the boys were occupied and fed, the meal was much more likely to go smoothly.

She sat for fifteen minutes, sipping her tea, before Angie arrived. "Jason is bringing the boys in after they go look at the pond."

"Good move," Irene agreed.

Angie looked her over, taking in her sling. "Typing too many spreadsheets?"

Irene laughed. "I took a fall and hurt my shoulder. I'll be fine in a few days."

Angie studied her. "Have you seen Jennifer today?"

Irene nodded. "I went to church with her."

"Did she buy that story?"

Irene gave her a stern look. "It's not a story. Don't

make a big deal about it or she'll go into concerned mother mode, and you know I hate that. I've been to see the doctor. I'll heal." She took a deep breath. "But, speaking of things I don't want Jennifer to know about, I need to tell you I can't babysit anymore."

Angie frowned. "I know we were late getting back home this week. The music was good, and we got carried away. It won't happen again."

"No. It's too much with my schedule." Irene's clipped response indicated there was no changing her mind.

At that moment, Jason and the boys entered the restaurant, followed by Jennifer. Irene's pre-ordering meant that for a few moments everyone was content. The waiter went around to take additional orders, and the group chatted over appetizers and helping the children with their food.

By the time the second round of orders appeared, Dave and Mike were done eating and ready to settle down with their e-pads. The adults ate, passing dishes and catching up on various events.

"Did you see that Irene hurt herself?" Jennifer commented.

"It's hard to miss, Jennifer," Angie remarked.

Jason looked startled, apparently not noticing before. He gave Irene a once-over. "You've got your arm in a sling."

Irene's smile was forced. "I fell."

"You were doing that dog thing again," Jennifer accused.

"I was at agility practice," Irene admitted.

"It's a silly waste of time. I've told you that."

Irene took a deep breath. "Yes, you have." One of

Jennifer's favorite lectures was on the time and money Irene wasted on "that dog" in a sport without "available men." Irene was not in the mood to hear it again.

"When did you fall?" Angie asked.

"Thursday night."

"Didn't you go to the doctor last week?"

"Yes. Annual physical."

Angie's head tilted. She was clearly suspicious, but after a moment she turned to Jason to ask about his weekly schedule. Jennifer continued to watch Irene.

Irene didn't meet Jennifer's gaze and went back to her pepper prawns.

****

Irene got home and set some water on the stove to boil. Sharon knocked a few moments later, coming in without waiting for Irene to call out permission. "Why did you leave?" she asked, worry clear on her face.

"Jennifer asked me to come to church," Irene responded.

"What did she want?"

"Nothing major. I think I spoiled her plans by being injured. Don't worry about it.

She sniffed. "How's your arm?"

"I'm sore, but I'm going to live. You don't need to worry."

"Hmmm." When the water boiled, Sharon went over and studied the tea choices. She chose a green tea, then added a powder she had brought with her.

"Nothing with marijuana." Irene warned, familiar with how alternative Sharon's medicine could be.

"It's arnica with alfalfa for the vitamin B."

"Yummy."

"Drink before you complain."

Irene took a sip. Sharon had added honey.

Sharon studied Irene for another few minutes. "I'm going to get my massage table."

"No. You don't need to do that. I'm on the mend."

"It'll give me a chance to tell you about my class last night." She left to run back to her house.

Fifteen minutes later Sharon was gently rubbing Irene's abused arm and telling her about the cooking class. "So, we all ended up making ginger stir fry with zucchini noodles."

"Mumm. That sounds good."

"It was."

They were both quiet for another few minutes before Sharon said, "Irene, I was thinking about adding an MS yoga class to my schedule. Maybe something that would be a group. I'm not sure. What do you think?"

As a licensed chiropractor, Sharon also performed reiki, massage, acupressure, and other types of holistic treatment at her practice. She was always handing out herbs and elixirs to people who she claimed had a bad aura or traumatic past life experiences.

When she started the center, it had been a one-room office. Then she started partnering with a yoga instructor, so they took a studio space. Then she added a massage therapist on staff. Then Pilates, tai chi, and classes on balance for the elderly. The center was now a large thriving complex. Irene had no idea how Sharon found time to keep abreast of it all, but she did. She was Irene's opposite in almost every way, but also her rock.

"I'm not sure. That's a big step."

"I know. I have several chiropractic customers with MS, and yoga is listed as a possibly beneficial exercise. In fact, I've been reading about it. Yoga has the potential to lessen several physical symptoms of MS and may contribute to improved strength, flexibility, posture, balance, focus, circulation, digestion, elimination, pelvic floor health and to decreased tension, fatigue, and spasticity. There's even a type of yoga that's supposed to be best. It's called adaptive yoga. There's a whole society in Michigan that does this."

"That's a big commitment. Are you sure there is enough interest?"

Sharon added more lotion to her hands. "I've been reading. MS is more common in women and people of northern European descent. The Pacific Northwest has a higher-than-average rate. Almost three thousand cases in Oregon alone."

"That's small when you think about how many people it would take to keep a class going."

"Maybe. But it sounds interesting to me."

"I can't commit."

"Okay, but think about it."

Chapter 23

Her arm still in its sling, Irene met Peter at the state car lot at seven a.m. before they headed up to Lakelynn. Overall, she was feeling better, but wished the day's meetings weren't necessary.

"Has everyone confirmed for ten?" she asked once they had picked up their coffee and were headed north.

Peter nodded. He checked the blind spot, then changed lanes to pass a slower moving tractor-trailer. "I don't think anyone was happy, but after Friday's events, they realize they don't have a choice."

On the previous Friday morning, while Irene was at urgent care with her injuries, *The Herald* had published a story about Lakelynn. The story landed on page three, below the fold. It described the audit delays and on-site presence of investigators from the OA. Mayor Lynda Sherry gave a melodramatic press conference which only fanned the flames, and sound bites made the evening news on every local affiliate.

Sunday's paper—which Irene read while recovering at home—featured a front-page article along with a photo of Lynda, hands in the air, mouth askew, clearly in the middle of a spirited tirade.

"Slim Down" Mayor Announces Possible Embezzlement
Friday – 10am
The mayor of Lakelynn, members of the city council,

and other city officials held a press conference late Thursday to announce possible embezzlement turned up by a state-dictated audit.

"I'm shocked and dismayed that any city employee could even contemplate taking tax-payer money," Mayor Lynda Sherry stated. The well-known and vocal critic of government waste went on to say, "It's a crying shame we have to rely on paid auditors to do what everyone should be doing automatically."

City Councilors Jayne Tanaka, Bill Henley, and Robert Austin offered no additional comments to the statement read by new city manager, Rusty Barrett.

"We regret to inform you that in the course of performing an annual audit, auditors have discovered discrepancies that lead us to believe some form of misappropriation of funds has happened. At this time, we are not prepared to discuss specifics, but we are working with the Oregon Office of Adjudication, Lakelynn Police, and Clackamas District Attorney's office as well as our auditors to determine the proper course of action."

Asked about when a perpetrator would be named, Barrett told reporters that it was a matter for the Clackamas District Attorney's office.

The Herald *was unable to reach the Oregon Office of Adjudication or Clackamas District Attorney's offices before publication deadline, but the public relations specialist for Lakelynn Police confirmed they were working with the other agencies.*

Irene took a sip of her coffee. "Did you have a chance to speak with Rusty?"

Peter nodded. "He confirmed no one expressed interest in our presence or reasons for being at city hall until Thursday, late in the day. He told me that after you and I left on Thursday afternoon, Betty made a big scene with the auditors. She got into one gal's face about a request for contract backup."

"Which contract?" Irene asked.

"He didn't say."

"Okay. We'll check it out. What happened next?"

Peter took a sip of his own coffee. "After Betty left, the auditor told Rusty that he was sure some of the contracts being paid didn't exist."

"Ahhh."

"From there, no one will admit what happened next. What we do know is that the mayor was in the office at the time of the hullabaloo. But the door to the conference room was open during part of the explosion, and Rusty admitted he didn't get it shut quickly enough because he was trying to calm Betty down."

Irene nodded.

"Friday morning, when Rusty came to work, there were three messages from reporters asking for more information on the audit. *The Herald* article was out, with an editor's note that they'd been unable to reach the anyone for comment."

"Convenient."

"Indeed. Rusty contacted the reporters who had left messages and downplayed the incident, referring back to the original press release. When the mayor arrived, Rusty couldn't talk her out of the press conference."

Irene blew out a breath and looked at the fields of hay lining I-5. "And we know the rest of that story."

"The auditor emailed us their initial report. We can go over it with the city council."

"I saw the email," Irene confirmed. "That's fast."

Peter agreed.

"And what did you learn, my young apprentice, from the files you worked on?"

"Young apprentice?" Peter said in horror.

"Patience you must have," she said in perfect deadpan.

"Not the voice," Peter begged. "I'll tell you everything, just not the voice."

"Fear is the path—"

"When I matched their contracts to the list of checks," Ignoring her chuckles, Peter spoke over her, "I was able to uncover about a dozen vendors without contracts. Now, that could be because the purchase was a low dollar amount or because the vendor's contract is old. But there were three vendors that I found intriguing."

"Intriguing? How?"

"All three have generic names. The kind that could mean anything. But when I looked them up online, I wasn't able to find any information."

"That's unusual."

"Indeed. I sent you a list: Silver Industries, Red Wren Services, and Willamette Falls Consulting."

"Red Wren Services wasn't online?" Irene asked in surprise. "Isn't that the big advertising agency that completed the advertising campaign for the state?"

Peter nodded slowly. "Yeah, I think that's them."

Irene got out her phone. "It's weird they don't have a contract on file. Spend some time today getting information about those three contracts. If we need to get a warrant for more information, let me know. We may be getting to that stage."

"Will do. What will you be doing?"

Irene sighed. "Dealing with the circus."

Peter broke the ensuing silence in the car. "I haven't asked about your arm because you usually don't want to talk about that kind of stuff."

Irene turned to look out the window. The fields had transformed into strip malls and chair stores. "Your instincts are sound, as usual."

He said nothing more for a few moments, then offered, "If you want to talk about it, I'll listen. And if you need help today, please let me know. Don't push yourself."

Irene nodded. "You know I've been having some medical problems, but I can handle this." She paused. "Can I give you a piece of advice in return?"

"Okay."

"Stay cool."

Their gazes locked.

"Poker face," they said in unison.

****

When they arrived at city hall, Rusty swept down on them. "Can I talk to you before you get going?" He waved his arms in the direction of his office, then paused, looking confused. "What happened to you?" He gestured toward her sling.

"I took a tumble over the weekend. I'll survive. Let's talk."

Rusty led the way to his office. They sat down in the visitor chairs and watched him tap his hands nervously along the desk blotter. "What's up?" Irene prompted.

He took a big sigh, then blurted, "Betty left a letter on my desk this morning. She's threatening to quit unless she's treated with more respect." He slid a piece of paper across the desk for Irene to read.

Rusty

Thank you for providing me with a copy of the fiscal auditor's requests. I wish that the state auditor demonstrated some professionalism and respected my rights and character on this issue rather than resorting to unfounded accusations, threat, harassment, and intimidation.

In defense of my credibility, let me first state that I have brought out many problems to the City of Lakelynn management when I took office as Finance Director. ironic and a travesty that instead of getting the support, I was critisized insulted and humiliated.

As I have reported, the finance software systems out of date. Because of various interference, the software upgrade scheduled for early 2015 was postponed. While the city's finance department is utilizing the financial software, without more staffing as well as the upgrade, we are not utilizing the full extent of the software. It was not through my negligence that this happened.

I find it ironic that it is only now that this is being recognized.

Thank you again for your professional and respect you have afforded me in this matter.

Irene pondered the letter for several moments. While the spelling and grammar mistakes were revealing, she couldn't understand how Betty had leaped to some of her conclusions or how Betty's "rights and character" had been disrespected. As well, she couldn't think of what she might have said that could be interpreted as "accusations, threat, harassment, and intimidation."

Was this a guilty conscience talking? Or the overreaction of an overworked leader?

"Rusty, an audit is an audit. No one is trying to

offend her. Audits don't change because she's upset."

"I know. I know." But he didn't say anything else.

Irene let the silence draw out, waiting for him to reveal his thoughts. "If that's all—" she began and rose.

Rusty stood as well, looking around the room vacantly.

"I'm going to head to the conference room to prepare for the meeting with the city council," she finally said. "See you there."

As she left, Rusty remained standing behind his desk.

Chapter 24

Irene and Peter hoped this would be a final meeting with the city council. They sat in the formal conference room with Rusty, Jayne Tanaka, Bill Henley, and Robert Austin. Mayor Lynda Sherry had not arrived yet.

Irene approached Robert Austin, whom she'd not met before. She held out her hand to him. "It's a good thing I'm right-handed," she said, wiggling the fingers of her left hand to indicate her sling.

"What happened?" Robert asked solicitously.

"I took a fall and landed wrong. I wish it was a better story."

He nodded, and they chatted for a moment about the weather.

Irene had dressed carefully for the day and noticed Jayne Tanaka had as well. Bill Henley had opted to dress as informally as he had at their first meeting. Rusty had upgraded his outfit to include a jacket and tie. As always, Peter was nattily attired with a fashionable bowtie; he could wear things like that and make them appear perfectly normal.

Robert Austin, however, wore a stylish suit whose tailored fit emphasized his trim build. Irene guessed his age to be mid-fifties, and his dark hair was smooth and coiffed. She thought he looked ready to step in front of the camera, then remembered Bill's comment about him only showing up when the press was expected.

Irene looked at her watch. "Well, let's hope Lynda gets here soon, but we might as well get started." Everyone shifted uncomfortably, but no one objected. Irene walked back to her seat.

"As I'm sure you saw over the weekend," she began, "the media have taken a sudden interest in this audit. However, that is not the primary reason for today's meeting." She took out a piece of paper. "A series of checks totaling over—" She looked down at her notes. "—$286,749.83 have been made out to non-existent vendors and cashed out of Lakelynn's bank account."

A stunned silence fell over the room. Finally, Jayne said, "You're sure?"

Irene nodded. "Late last week, we confirmed that the cash and check reconciliations have been tampered with. We went through the vendors and were able to confirm the fraud."

"Who is it?" Bill asked.

The door to the conference room crashed open. Lynda Sherry stomped into the room and flopped into an empty chair. "I don't appreciate the lack of notice I was given about this meeting."

Irene studied her.

With considerably less calm, Jayne snapped, "Oh, for God's sake, Lynda. They sent us a message on Friday. That's hardly a lack of notice."

"I had appointments I couldn't reschedule," Lynda said haughtily.

Bill said abruptly, "I'd like to hear more about what Irene told us."

Irene looked around the room, being sure to meet each person's eyes. "As I said, we can confirm almost $300,000 has been siphoned from the city's accounts."

Lynda came out of her chair with a shriek. "What?"

Raising her good hand, Irene cut her off. "I was about to explain."

Lynda sat back in her chair, clearly unsettled, but quiet for the moment.

"When the private auditor pointed out to Peter and me that the bank reconciliations had been tampered with, we were able to target certain payments and check them against contracts as well as against known companies. We narrowed it down to three probable companies." Irene paused to let her words sink in. "We compared those companies to the actual bank records, and it wasn't long before the pattern became clear."

"And what is that pattern?" Jayne asked.

"All of the checks are made out to Willamette Falls Consulting. That's clever. It's a name that could mean anything in this area, but it's not tied to a particular person. Whoever is behind this knows how financial systems work, particularly the systems here. The amounts are never above the one-thousand-dollar limit, which requires a personal signature. The checks go out once a month. At first glance, anyone checking would think they look like a regular bill or consulting fee."

Peter spoke up. "The culprit could have simply run the checks, but they went to great lengths to adjust the bank statements and to piggyback the amounts onto an existing contract." He looked at his notes. "The contract for Red Wren Services has been consistently drained, with the checks for that contract being the same checks that were adjusted on the banking statements."

"Red Wren Services?" Robert asked. "The public relations firm?

Peter nodded.

"Why did we hire them?" Bill asked. "And when?"

"The contract was ratified seven years ago," Peter said with a shrug. "Originally, the city wanted them to handle a bond measure, then the contract was revised to address the high school construction messaging. Recently, the contract was revised again to cover—" He paused, struggling for a polite euphemism. "— personnel and management challenges."

"You mean the former mayor," Jayne said flatly.

Irene took over for Peter. "We have been unable to find any record of a company by the name of Willamette Falls Consulting. That doesn't prove anything, but it's obvious that someone is using the company to systematically drain funds." She looked around the room. The expressions ranged from stunned to terrified.

"It's going to take some time before we have all the details," she stated. "This meeting is to apprise you of developments and to inform you that we will have to do more interviews, specifically that we will be interviewing all of you."

"Interview us?" Lynda screeched. "What do you mean, interview us? *We* clearly didn't have anything to do with this."

"This is standard," Irene said. "Our role is now to find the embezzler and stop them. I've been in touch with my boss at the OA, as well as the state attorney. I will next meet with the district attorney to apprise them of the situation."

"Why are you bringing more people into this?" Lynda wailed.

"The jurisdiction to prosecute any wrongdoing is tricky. My boss asked me to speak to the DA to ensure they were up to date." Irene kept her demeanor calm.

"Well, I think you should keep your mouth shut!" Lynda snapped. "I'm going to get my lawyer." She glared at Rusty. "This is what comes of bringing in the OA. They can't wait to get everyone under their thumb."

She turned to the room at large. "In fact, I think we should talk about whether or not we want Rusty to continue. I move we cancel his contract."

"Enough." Jayne snapped. "Nothing is on the table except damage control. And, Lynda, if you can't pull it together and be a professional, I'll get the police to come over here and arrest you for disturbing the peace"

Quietly, Bill said, "*The Herald* knows something is up. It's only a matter of time before someone starts talking to them."

"Let's all calm down," Robert huffed. "I'm not sure we should be talking like this in front of everyone." It was clear that the "everyone" was Rusty.

Rusty stiffened. "My job is to protect the city, and I'm going to give it my best shot. The first thing is to draft a statement to the staff and the press. We need to keep the union apprised and working with us, otherwise that will become its own set of problems."

The room was quiet. Even Lynda.

"This," Bill said heavily, "is a great big pile of shit."

Irene rose from her chair. "I need to be going to my next appointment." She distributed business cards to everyone in the room. "I am available to answer questions, though I may need to check with my superiors about how much information I will be able to release. I need to emphasize that things are far from settled, and the best thing to do is to stay calm and come up with a plan."

Jayne nodded. "Okay. Thank you for your time and

for being frank with us." She looked around the room with the air of a commander gathering her troops. "Rusty's right. It's time to steer this ship. Can everyone stay here for the next few hours to get some work done?"

"No problem for me," Bill said.

"I can stay," said Lynda. "But I don't think this is necessary."

Robert shifted. "I need to get back to the office."

"Robert, if you leave, I swear I'll let it leak that you were MIA for this whole thing," Jayne warned.

"I'd like to stay, too," said Rusty.

"All right." Jayne turned to Irene. "Do you have a report or something of that nature which we can look at to make sure we get our facts straight?"

Irene offered a report Peter had drafted. "These are my notes for this meeting."

Jayne took them. "Thank you for your time. Please keep us abreast of the latest news."

Irene and Peter left the room. Silently, they walked down the hall to find a quiet space.

"Thoughts?" Irene asked, once they found a private area and were seated at a small table.

"I didn't think it was one of them before, and I don't see any reason to think it's them now. But"—Peter shook his head—"I'm not sure how they are going to get through this. They seem clueless."

Irene sighed. "If it is one of them, they are better actors than I thought." She took out her legal pad. "Can you stay here the rest of the day to see if we can connect any more dots? I'm going to meet with the district attorney next."

"Can you drive with that sling?" Peter asked doubtfully.

"I'll be careful," Irene responded. "Can you find out how much longer the audit will take?"

"I spoke to the auditors before the meeting. They had two weeks scheduled for field work, then two more to finalize the opinion." Peter frowned. "They weren't happy with additional time here, but they're adjusting their schedule."

"Okay." Irene made a note. "What's the status on getting new check stock to pay the bills?"

"The bank had issued a new set of accounts. They've already got new check stock. The purchasing cards will have to be reissued. The auditors are working with Rusty to set up a more secure check inventory system."

Irene made more notes. "Has the auditor completed staff interviews?"

"They have some follow-up, but payroll looks good. The AR/AP departments look good, in spite of everything else. They are doing their jobs; it's the higher-ups who aren't following the rules."

"Except for that pesky $286,000," Irene said dryly.

"Except for that," Peter agreed.

Irene closed her legal pad, leaned back in her chair slightly, and smiled at Peter. "Who do you think it is?"

He laughed. "If I told you, that would be cheating."

"Indeed."

Peter turned serious. "Watch your back, Irene. Lynda has political traction. She may be able to make your life harder than you bargain for."

"Maybe I can do the same for her."

****

Irene entered the glass doors of the Clackamas County offices and walked across the lobby to the information desk. She was directed to the fourth floor to meet Assistant District Attorney Gary Boyd. The fourth-floor receptionist told her that Mr. Boyd would be another few minutes. Irene took a seat and fished out some pain killers from her bag; her shoulder ached in spite of the sling.

As she had expected, the state's attorney deferred to the local district attorney for the warrants that would allow access to the deposit and routing information for Willamette Falls Consulting.

Things would move slowly and carefully because the jurisdiction in this kind of case was complicated. Usually, cities allowed the next higher form of government to take over criminal prosecution, for the simple reason they did not have the apparatus to try cases. The state and county both wanted things to be clearer before they committed to a course of action. If the City of Lakelynn decided to pursue civil charges, they were the only party who could bring those charges.

Gary Boyd came out within minutes. Irene realized she had met him before at some function. He was an average-looking man of about forty. His suit was well-cut, but not slick. His blond hair could be described as sandy rather than sun kissed. She remembered thinking he had an attractive aura of intelligence about him. It was impossible not to notice that he was missing one leg; his prosthetic ankle was visible above his shoe. Still, he walked smoothly and didn't ask anyone to comment on his condition.

"Thank you for meeting me so quickly," Irene said, extending her right hand.

He shook it gently. "I hope your sling comes with a good story." He possessed a charming smile, which helped in the attraction department.

Irene smiled back. "I wish. I took a fall. Thank you for meeting with me today."

"Always happy to help a lady with dog hair on her skirt."

Irene brushed at her skirt, embarrassed.

He made a dismissive motion. "I've probably got enough dog hair on my suit to start a whole new animal. Let's go to my office."

In his office, Irene took him up on his offer of tea, then gave him a brief outline of the events to date while he brewed it. "Mr. Boyd, we need to get some warrants to continue building a case, and I'd rather move ahead with the DA's knowledge."

Boyd nodded. "The amount is nearly three hundred thousand?"

"Yes."

"Would we be in a position to ever get the money back?"

"It's possible, but usually little is recovered."

"Yes." A moment passed. "We need to be seen as doing something proactive."

"Mr. Boyd, public relations is not my forte."

He smiled. "Fair enough. I assume you won't mind if I have our staff work on it?"

Irene shook her head. "That's fine. Depending on how you want to handle it, the city has their PR team working on it. I think their work has been solid, but there are other factors at work."

Gary smiled slightly. "I think I've met the mayor a couple of times." He studied his notes. "I'm not sure I've met the city manager. I've met the council members. Who else should I know about?"

Irene thought about it. "Both my colleague and I think the problem is inside the finance department. If we're right, the scam has been going on for years. That limits the possibilities, but rooting out the problem could be messy."

"Okay. Let's get some warrants for those checks. I'll file the necessary papers and talk to my superiors. Do you want to pursue criminal charges, regardless of circumstances?"

Irene sighed. "Ultimately, the city will have to decide that. But it's usually considered best practice to bring charges against the embezzler. It signals the city is a victim but trying to get the money back."

He sighed. "Okay. I know Robert Austin pretty well. I can't say I like him, but I know him. I'll call him and suggest some proactive measures."

Irene nodded, hiding her surprise. Most of the time, the conversation focused on next prosecutorial steps, not how to make the city look better. Her respect for Boyd grew.

"I'm even worse at politics than I am at public relations," she started.

He smiled. "But…"

"In my years doing this, I have honestly never seen such a dysfunctional situation. The mayor is a loose canyon. The council is MIA. The city manager is either too nice for the job or not qualified. I'd hate to see you try to help the situation and get mowed down by the runaway train."

He smiled at her. Their eyes met for a long moment.

She broke the moment by glancing at her watch. "I need to pick up my co-worker and head back home." She handed Gary her business card. "Let me know when you get the warrants. I'll do the next few steps from Salem. I'll probably be back in the middle of next week, but if you need me, I can make arrangements to come back up sooner."

He took her hand. "I'll be in touch."

"Thank you for your help."

Again, he smiled. "Anytime."

Chapter 25

Irene chose to go to her Salem office on Tuesday to wait for more information—and dodge the media which had exploded.

Lakelynn Laments

By Kenneth Margolis

The blows keep coming for the town of Lakelynn. Last week senior officials announced possible irregularities had been uncovered by a state-mandated audit. Yesterday sources confirmed the auditors were estimating the embezzled amount was at least six figures. Mayor Lynda Sherry has not made a comment on the matter since Friday. On Monday evening, The Herald attempted to obtain confirmation of the stolen amount but was unable to reach the mayor or members of the city council. Similarly, the Oregon Office of Adjudication and the auditors of record were unavailable for comment. Even the city's public relations coordinator simply said the city will be issuing a statement soon.

Irene scanned the first few paragraphs of the front-page story, but it was nothing new. Rusty had told her that reporters from every major news station were parked in front of city hall and the phones were ringing off the hook. She could believe it. Press had begun calling the OA office late yesterday afternoon to such a point the front desk receptionist had to request backup for phone duty. Evidence to resolve the case was not coming swiftly. Peter began to work with the bank, but they were not helpful. They wanted a warrant, then a lawyer to go over the warrant. It all took time.

Irene briefed her boss on all that had transpired before heading to her general practitioner for a follow-up on her shoulder. She was already feeling better, but it was easier to go than argue with Sharon. From the doctor's visit, she returned to the office and got to work.

Peter called her after lunch. "I got it," he crowed. "Every one of the Willamette Falls Consulting checks was deposited into an account that is listed as belonging to Willamette Falls Consulting. The contact information for the account is a disconnected phone number and a P.O. box. All of the checks were deposited in the night drop and marked 'for deposit only.' Within two weeks, the money would be e-transferred to an account, listed as WFC at Axos Banking. I've already contacted DA Boyd to get the warrants."

"Did he say when they'd come through?"

"Tomorrow. Maybe."

"Axos is online only, right?" Irene turned to her computer to look them up. "Their headquarters are in California, so at least we won't have to do the international thing."

Peter didn't comment for a moment. "You know who it is, don't you?"

"I've got a fair idea. We'll go slowly and collect more evidence. The bigger problem is we've got at least two scams going on."

"Two?"

She nodded, though Peter couldn't see it. "Willamette Falls Consulting is the first, but I'm certain that Betty and Lynda are systematically manipulating the revenue. I can't find any evidence that they are siphoning money, but I'm sure they are maneuvering entries to back up the mayor's theories."

"Why bother to do all that if they aren't getting any money out of it?" Peter wondered.

"She wants to be governor. I guess she thinks showing additional revenue as well as lower expenses will get her there."

"Is it against the law to adjust revenue but not take any money?"

"Public fiduciaries have an absolute obligation to put the public's interest before their own direct or indirect personal interests. As elected, appointed, employed, or volunteer public officials, they are subject to the Oregon Government Ethics law as set forth in ORS Chapter 244. Of course, that only guarantees civil penalties, but it's a start."

Peter said nothing.

"I'm open to suggestions," Irene said.

"I'll let you know when I have one."

"Me, too."

Irene was moody and on edge as she went back to her regular duties by scheduling interviews for other cases, caught up on emails, and reviewed reports. Periodically, she'd research an idea, but nothing came together.

Lakelynn was not her only case. She looked over a request for an audit of the superintendent of a school district from the Clatsop County District Attorney. The school had already done an audit and had found a bunch of suspicious activity; they wanted the OA to review the case and recommend their next action. The superintendent, who had been there for over twenty years, was well known and liked by everyone. The school district was not anxious to proceed without covering their bases.

Her laptop dinged, informing her that Peter had forwarded an email from the bank manager with more information about the Willamette Falls Consulting account. The account had been opened in 1998. There had been little or no activity on the account, which had remained at a balance of over five hundred dollars, until 2012. Then a small but steady stream of deposits began, with matching electronic withdrawals a few days to a week later. This pattern continued until 2015 when activity had picked up. The deposits were now thousands instead of hundreds, but always night-dropped checks. The balance remained steady; there were no fees and only occasional activity. Even the account maintenance went to an email address, so the account was paperless.

He had also followed up on the P.O. box, which was located at a private postal business. The owner was reluctant to share specifics without a warrant, but had admitted the box had changed hands several times over the years. Irene was trying to decide whether to request a warrant. Banks are required to have a physical address to open an account, but the account had been opened so long ago, the P.O. box was grandfathered in. The bank reported they made annual attempts to get updates, but they had been ignored.

In late afternoon, Peter swung by her desk. "The second bank got back to us. It's the same pattern as the other one. The money goes in and is electronically transferred to another account."

"At the same bank?" Irene asked without hope.

"Nope. But this bank has a physical presence, and the transfers have a last name registered to the receiving account—Moore."

Irene quickly flipped through her mental files. "I don't think we've met a Moore."

Peter shook his head. "I looked it up. No Moore is employed at Lakelynn."

"Have you already contacted the DA?"

He nodded.

Irene pondered the top of her desk for a moment. "Okay. Let me know if there are any more updates."

After Peter left, Irene rubbed her neck. She hated to let this drag out, but if she tried to push it forward, it would mean they would have to do the interviews without proof. That meant they had to wait.

Chapter 26

Irene didn't arrive home until well after five, but for her, that made it a short day. She felt drained and her arm ached like an infected tooth. She dutifully changed clothes and took Percy for a stroll around the neighborhood. He made her smile, enjoying himself by inspecting all the smells, tail wagging softly.

After they returned home, she prepared a salad, slicing an extra measure of vegetables for Percy who supervised with rapt interest. She sat down to eat, the latest from her favorite mystery author propped in back of the plate, when a car pulled up in the driveway. Percy clambered out of his bed and ran over to the big window. Irene followed him to the window.

When she saw Angie climb out of the car, Irene suddenly felt even more tired than she had a moment ago. Angie hadn't called to ask to come over. She entered without knocking, gave Percy a cursory pet, and bellowed, "I'm so angry with Jason."

"Hello, Angie," Irene said, struggling for patience. Angie was dressed for her job as sales manager, her high heels and short skirt contrasting with Irene's simple at-home wear.

"I'm so angry with him," her sister reiterated, marching to the cupboard and pulling down a glass which she filled with something she found in the refrigerator.

Irene forked up a bite of salad. "Why are you angry with Jason?" she asked dutifully, then inserted the greens into her mouth and chewed. Of course, Angie was going to tell Irene whether she wanted to know or not.

"He took an extra shift every day this week and didn't tell me. I thought he would be home, so I didn't schedule a babysitter in the evenings. Now, I'm supposed to snap my fingers and take care of it. Heaven knows, he can't be bothered to pick up a phone."

Angie had met Jason when she was seventeen; he had been twenty-five, and Irene had always considered him the more immature of the two. While Angie and Jason had been together for nine years, and married for seven, their relationship was tumultuous. Arguments escalated to one party spending the night in a hotel. Days later, the pair would be detained for public lewdness at a music festival.

It wasn't just their relationship that was chaotic, it was their entire lives. Six weeks after Mike had been born, Jason decided he would take a commercial fishing job in Alaska. They packed up within days and left at three in the morning so they could drive there in time for him to get on the next boat.

Angie followed every time Jason decided to change careers. Skateboard manufacturing, tourism guide, oil maverick. They had been in the Willamette Valley now for three years, and Irene could see the signs of restlessness.

In some ways, the relationship had been a steadying influence on her sister. Seeing the need to bring in an income, Angie took a car sales job. She'd stayed with the same auto group for her entire career. While the field was male dominated, she had done well. In the last few years, she had steadily climbed the management ladder of the large auto group.

"Don't even think that I'm going to offer," Irene warned.

Angie sighed and flopped into a chair across from her. "No. I never even considered it. I'll find someone. He makes me crazy."

Irene studied her dubiously. "So, why are you here?"

"Can't I swing by to talk to my sister?"

"You could," Irene agreed. "But we both know you didn't." She took another bite of salad.

Angie took a drink. "What's going on with you?"

Irene stopped chewing for a moment, then started again. She swallowed before responding. "What do you mean?"

"You've been going to the doctor all the time," Angie said, ticking off points on her finger. "You've lost weight. You turn up to Sunday lunch bruised and with your arm in a sling. You can't babysit."

"Ah, the real point of concern comes out," Irene said bitterly. "I have my own life, you know."

Angie continued. "I've seen your hands tremble. You've had some memory lapses. A few weeks ago, you told me you felt dizzy."

"Everyone feels dizzy occasionally," Irene said defensively.

"What's going on?" Angie repeated softly.

Irene felt a surge of anger she couldn't quite explain. "Angie, it's been a long day. I don't want to get into this tonight."

"Well, at least you didn't deny it and say it was nothing."

Irene took a bit of salad and chewed it belligerently. Angie remained calm, a seasoned negotiator. Irene took another bite; her jaw was so tense she was amazed she could open her mouth. She swallowed again.

"Let me get this straight," Irene began. She heard her voice, her tone, and hated herself for not being able to control it. "I can't drop everything or stay out until midnight babysitting your children, and suddenly there is something wrong with me."

Angie took a deep breath, visibly shaken. "I don't care about that; I'm concerned about you. Dave told me you fell when you took them hiking a few weeks ago. You keep saying you're tired. You—"

"I tripped and had a few sleepless nights!"

"Why are you acting like I am accusing you of something?" Angie exclaimed in bewilderment. "I'm worried. Even Jennifer mentioned—"

"Oh, great. Jennifer has decided there is something else that needs to be fixed."

Angie immediately came to their mother's defense. "You're too hard on her. She's worried."

"Classic. That's just so classic."

Irene stood up to carry her plate to the sink. She scooped the leftover vegetables into Percy's dish, and he responded enthusiastically. Her hand suddenly didn't want to close, and she dropped the dish. She cursed.

"I suppose you two were out together, shopping at the outlets or whatever, and she decided to check 'worry about Irene' off her annual list."

Angie was starting to flounder. "You're not making sense. We're worried and we want to support you."

"Support me?" Irene scoffed. "Don't make me laugh. It's about what the two of you need. She needs an accountant and cannot understand why I won't help her. And buy a bigger house. And find a rich husband. Or at least get married. And you," she said, stubbornly ignoring the hurt look on her sister's face, "I can't remember the last time you called without needing something. Babysitter? Character reference for a new house to rent? One hundred dollars? Just until the end of the month."

Silence fell over the room. With a sigh, Percy left his dog dish and escaped into the living room.

"I'm sorry you feel this way," Angie said quietly. "I didn't realize we were asking so much of you."

"You don't realize?" Irene said sarcastically. "Of course, you didn't. I work sixty hours a week and still take the boys out almost every weekend. I show up at church, which is more than you do. I can't remember the last time either of you asked how my job was going. Or how Percy and I did in a dog trial. Or even if I read a good book lately." The last words were spoken at such a volume that Percy returned to the kitchen, barking in excitement.

Visibly upset, Angie gathered up her keys and took a few steps to the door. Then she turned. "You're right. We don't ask about you. Because when we do, you blow us off. 'It's fine' should be carved above your mantel like some kind of ancient creed. I'll take the blame for not pushing harder. But it's a two-way street, Irene. You can't hide everything and refuse every offer of assistance and then blame us for not being a bigger part in your life."

Chapter 27

It took a few days before Irene and Peter had what they needed. Thursday morning, they returned to Lakelynn City Hall. Though her left arm was still in a sling, Irene had dressed in a sharp modern suit. She sat across from Betty Hacher, who was in her usual uniform of a wide-strapped tank top and jeans.

"Let's get this over with," Betty muttered. She had resisted returning for this interview, claiming she had no further responsibility since she had resigned. After Irene threatened to have the police bring her for an interview at the police station, she reluctantly agreed to meet them at the city buildings. But she wasn't happy about it.

Peter, also dressed formally, pulled a copy of the Willamette Falls Consulting invoice from his bag and slid it across the table.

"Tell me about that," Irene prompted.

Betty took the paper. "What about it? It's an invoice."

"It's an invoice that has been paid by the City of Lakelynn to a vendor without a contract. The vendor has no address or public information we can find."

The bluster dropped. "What?" Betty whispered. She looked as if a doctor had told her she had cancer.

Irene tapped the paper. "This is a copy of an invoice to Willamette Falls Consulting. It appears to have been approved by someone at the Public Works department.

It's been coded to the sidewalk fund." She took a breath. "As you can see, the check amount is under the amount required for signature. A stamp has been used to endorse the payment."

Peter slid a second piece of paper to Irene, who continued. "This invoice was paid from the City of Lakelynn's bank account. It was stamped 'for deposit only' and deposited into an account registered to Willamette Falls Consulting, Inc. We've traced several account transfers, each with an assumed name. A sophisticated scheme. But I never thought you were dumb, Betty."

Betty studied the invoice, then the check. "I have no memory of ever seeing a bill with that name on it."

"And you don't remember seeing it when you reconciled the bank records?"

Clearly irritated, Betty glanced up at Irene. "Obviously not."

"Because what we've also found out is that these checks were hidden from the reconciliation process by doctoring the bank records. Someone combined the amount of that check with another invoice on the bank records to hide the transaction."

Peter placed a fresh set of bank statements on the table between the two women. Little flags marked the relevant transactions.

"These are directly from the bank," Irene said. "You never saw these. You worked from downloaded statements."

Betty's gaze was riveted to the bank statements.

"Tell me how you didn't catch this, Betty. Because right now, I do not understand."

"Neither do I," Betty murmured. "We're so careful

about spending money."

Without sympathy, Irene parried. "Not careful enough. Or maybe you've been too focused on saving pennies to notice the big picture."

Betty shook her head in confusion.

"It's someone with access to check stock and the bank statements," Irene said. "That's Kathy Nicols, Rusty Barrett, and you."

"It can't be her," Betty murmured. "She'd never waste the money."

"It can't be…who?" Irene asked.

Betty's hands trembled as she picked up the invoice. "I gave the mayor a key to the check stock."

"When?"

"A few months ago. Maybe four. She said she wanted to help us keep track of spending."

"How would giving Mayor Sherry access to the check stock help that?"

Betty started crying and soon was struggling to breathe through the choked tears.

Irene handed her a tissue from a box in the corner, then moved the box to the table between them. "Tell me what's going on, Betty."

Nodded frantically, Betty continued sobbing. Irene handed her a tissue. Minutes passed before she was able to speak. "Right after Lynda was elected, she took me out to lunch. She knew things weren't settled in the department, but that she wanted to help. We talked about Rusty. He had just started, but neither of us was sure he was up to the job. I told her I was feeling overwhelmed and that we needed to be able to hire some positions."

"What did she say to that?" Irene asked.

"She told me she understood. That we'd be able to

bring some more people on once the other departments realized how far they could tighten the belt. We'd get the spending down and then take a look at what needed to be addressed."

For the first time, Peter spoke. "Did she mention which other departments?"

Betty shook her head. "A few weeks later, she invited me out to drinks after a bad day at work. She told me I was doing a great job and that I shouldn't let it get me down. We talked about a few of the ongoing financial issues. We talked about how the council was fighting her vision, and she told me that I could help her out with that."

"How?" Irene asked.

"Rusty was new when the budget went through. The last finance manager was actually the one who had prepared most of it. He and Lynda didn't get on well. She told me that he had resisted making any of her changes. And then Rusty told her that he wasn't comfortable making changes and wanted to present the budget as prepared. He told her that he'd do what he could to support any changes she wanted to make by presenting them to the council."

Betty took a deep breath. "I helped prepare the budget, and Lynda knew I understood the process." She paused, biting her lip, then continued. "She suggested a new revenue allocation plan."

"Is that why there is so much income shifting going on?" Irene needed clarification.

Betty looked away. "Yes. It didn't take me long to realize that by putting revenue where she wanted it, rather than the areas it was budgeted, we were constantly having to take money out of the storage accounts."

"Why did she want it done this way?" Irene asked.

"Lynda said that if the subaccount balances were low, the program managers wouldn't want to spend money. They'd bend over backwards to save money. The money would be available if they needed it, but otherwise, we'd be saving money."

"And you didn't foresee problems?" Peter asked, unable to remain silent.

Betty looked down at her hands. "It didn't sound so bad when she suggested it. Like we were delaying expenses."

"But instead, you were hiding revenue," Irene stated.

She nodded. "A couple of months ago, I told her I was going to change everything back, but that we would still have to ask for a big adjustment at the year end. I asked her to explain to the council."

"And she wouldn't," Irene stated again.

Betty nodded again. "I got the budget changes ready, but she wouldn't allow them to go to the council. She said it was silly to waste their time on that. She told me to put the money where we needed it, but to keep as much of it in the general fund as possible."

"So, it looks like the general fund has extra dollars, even though other funds are overspent," Irene summarized.

Betty blinked. "Well, I wouldn't put it that way."

Irene and Peter exchanged a look.

Revenue manipulation was commonly used to make companies appear more profitable than they were. Governmental entities didn't make a profit, but showing extra funds was a good way to curry political favor.

By billing grants for funds spent, then entering that

cash into the general fund, Betty and the mayor were creating the appearance of prosperity. In the meantime, the unpaid bills were left as liabilities in obscure funds and projects. If anyone looked at these smaller funds, Betty could claim they were behind on billing. Vendors were left holding the bag, while interest accrued in the city's accounts. The vendors were eventually paid, but that was delayed as long as possible.

All of this allowed the mayor to take credit with her cost-cutting measures if anyone asked why the city had so much extra money.

But the city did not have any extra money. The manipulation worked over any given amount of time, but over the long term, the delayed liabilities caught up with the "extra money." This most usually happened when vendors started to add fees and interest to unpaid bills.

"When the public works manager came over to complain about the storm water program a couple months ago, this was the problem?" Irene correlated.

Betty nodded, taking over the story. "We got a federal grant to do some storm water work. The mayor said to draw down as much as we could and get it in the bank so we could get some interest. Public Works didn't get the proper approvals on the contracts, so we delayed paying the bills. When he got everything sorted out, he went online to do some reporting. The grant system showed we didn't have the money available, and he got upset."

"Did Kathy Nichols know about all this?" Irene asked.

"No," Betty denied. "Lynda told me that this should be between us. There are several people who do federal draw downs, but I'm the one who approves the coding when the cash comes in. I thought I would hear about it when Public Works was close to needing the cash."

"And then you'd move the money back?"

"Yes. I was keeping track of all that. But things started getting out of control. It got to be huge amounts and other project managers were complaining. I needed Lynda to approach the council and explain the plan so we could make a big journal entry and fix everything." She said this as though repeating the end of a fairy tale. Irene expected her to end with *and they lived happily ever after*.

Irene continued to study Betty. Finally, she broke the silence by asking, "How much of all this does Rusty Barrett know?"

"None. He didn't need to know. He's been busy putting out other fires and trying to keep the mayor out of city business. I was going to get him to help me do the budget modifications this year and then we'd be all squared away. No harm, no foul."

"What about those pesky cash shortages?" Irene said dryly.

"I wouldn't call them cash shortages," Betty temporized, attitude returning. "We didn't have the money where it needed to be."

Irene closed her eyes briefly and prayed for patience. She didn't feel like debating semantics. "Is Willamette Falls Consulting part of this whole thing?"

"No. I've never even heard of them before you arrived."

Irene ignored her increasingly cynical voice. "You never saw an invoice? Heard someone mention it?"

Betty's gaze was steady. "No."

Irene wrote something on a pad and passed it to

Peter. He nodded. Betty looked flustered.

Peter took over. "Let's move on. Is there anyone in the office that you've heard talking about unusual life changes? Buying an extra house? A new car?"

Betty thought about it. "No. Rose and her husband have a beach house, but they've had that for years. Kathy bought a luxury sedan a few months ago. I was surprised, but she said her husband helped with the down payment."

"Has anyone had a fatal illness in the family?" Irene pressed. "Lots of medical bills?"

Betty shook her head. "No. Nothing unusual. I've had a tough year with arthritis. Our receptionist had carpal tunnel surgery a few months ago." She laughed weakly. "We've been too busy to have a medical emergency."

They let Betty leave. Irene got up from her chair and stretched. Peter used a creative Anglo-Saxon phrase.

"I think she's incompetent," Peter summarized. "But I don't think she's our embezzler."

Irene nodded. "No, she's not."

Chapter 28

As Irene and Peter entered the conference room to meet with the city council members, she experienced a sense of *déjà vu*. She settled herself in the chair, intensely aware they were once again waiting for Mayor Lynda Sherry.

Lynda arrived at the meeting without her usual confident swagger, but her attitude was far from cowed. On the contrary, she had a chip on her shoulder. *A good offense makes the best defense*, thought Irene.

Everyone looked exhausted, as though they were at the end of the day, instead of approaching lunch. But Irene also noticed the determined square of Rusty Barrett's shoulders and the resolute set of Jayne Tanaka's jaw and smiled inwardly.

The gloves were about to come off.

"Lynda," Jayne began, "we've asked you to meet with us today out of courtesy—"

"Courtesy." she scoffed. "I'm the mayor. This is exactly where I should be."

"We are offering you the courtesy," Jayne repeated, "of hearing this directly. The council commissioned this audit. Your presence is far from mandatory."

Lynda looked like she wanted to argue but chose to hold her tongue.

"Irene, please start us off," Jayne invited.

Irene stood. "As you know, a private firm was hired

to do a general audit and get the city up to date with state reporting requirements. Their focus was on standard financial audit issues such as reporting and accounting procedures."

She stopped, waiting for the room to catch up. "The OA was contacted before the private auditors could start because there were concerns about missing check stock." Irene nodded to Rusty. "It quickly became apparent that the city was facing several challenges."

Peter pointed to a slide he was projecting onto a screen. "Those irregularities fell into two groups: Embezzlement and fraud."

"Why are those in two separate categories?" Jayne asked, clearly confused.

Irene stepped in. "We know someone has been taking money, which is the embezzlement. The fraud is a series of systematic"— She paused, searching for the correct words. —"questionable decisions that benefit someone in non-monetary ways."

"We hope to catch the embezzler by the end of the day," Peter said. "The fraud has been harder to pin down. At first, we thought it was part of the embezzlement pattern. In reality, the two issues are separate."

Irene looked around the room, meeting the foggy gazes of a leadership team that had been through too much.

"As you know, Lynda has strong opinions on how the government should be run. She ran on a platform of cutting government waste and shrinking taxes. Once she became mayor, she was determined to fulfil her campaign promises.

"She soon discovered that budgets and spending are more complicated than they appear. She couldn't tell the council how to spend or make a budget, and she couldn't command the city employees to overlook their duties and do what she wanted."

Lynda gave Irene a disgusted glare. "I was elected to fix the system."

Irene continued. "When Jayne had to take a leave from the council, Lynda saw her chance. She strong-armed Betty Hacher into a leadership role, then manipulated her into preparing budget documents that would allow her changes to have the maximum effect. Robert Austin, a newer council member, simply presented the budget without review.

"Once the budget was in place, instead of following it and placing revenue in the appropriate funds, Lynda worked with Betty to dump as much into the general fund as possible, at the same time billing out every grant and program fund. The net effect was a huge but deceptive jump in unrestricted general funds at the expense of the debts collecting in the restricted funds."

Insolently, Lynda rolled her eyes at Jayne. "I haven't taken over anything. We've obviously been reporting revenue." She looked around the table at the other councilors. "Last month we increased the general fund by ten percent and decreased expenses by fourteen percent. That's what makes a good leader."

"A leader who has encouraged city personnel to overlook generally accepted accounting principles," Irene said quietly. "A leader who now has burdened the taxpayers with thousands in late fees and federal reporting penalties."

"I've never embezzled!" Lynda shouted.

"We're not talking about the embezzlement," Irene said calmly. "That's a separate issue."

Lynda looked startled. "So, what are you accusing me of?"

Irene studied her in pity. "Like Peter said, we have two separate issues going on."

Lynda tossed her head and attempted to look down her nose at Irene. "You can't confuse me. I've been in business for thirty years and I've handled tougher opponents than you."

Irene shook her head, then turned back to Jayne. "We interviewed Betty Hacher this morning and she, reluctantly, outlined how she has been working with the mayor. I believe Betty didn't understand the severity of what she was doing, though she should have. My first recommendation is that you remove Betty from her position with the city."

She tapped a folder that sat in front of her. "Betty also told us that Lynda blocked necessary budget changes that would have allowed the finance department to correct the budget and reduce the accruing liabilities in those restricted fund accounts."

"We don't need budget changes," Lynda growled.

Peter interrupted. "The budget is your approval to spend money. If programs don't have the authority to spend and they do, the city is out of compliance."

"That's ridiculous. I'm the mayor. If I say it's okay for something to be spent, surely, it's fine. That's why the voters elected me."

"No, Lynda," Jayne snapped. "You still have to follow the rules. Shut up and let the rest of us hear the end of this."

"Bitch," Lynda said, the word loud enough that everyone could hear, but quiet enough that it was plausible she had been trying to withhold the insult.

"The private auditors will provide their own report," Peter explained. "Even without this situation, the city has serious funding problems. The new school construction is massively over budget and the bond has been spent to cover other debts."

"Is that even legal?" Jayne breathed.

"It's nothing," Lynda roared. "I told Betty to use the bond money to pay other bills to avoid paying interest on debt. The cash was right there."

Irene turned to look at her. "You encouraged Betty to use the money illegally."

"No. I encouraged her to use the money wisely."

"And what about the federal grant to do the stormwater work? You told Betty to draw down as much as you could, as fast as you could, so you could earn interest on the money."

"It's our money. Why shouldn't we earn interest on it? That's what the feds do. They rake in the interest by only giving us little portions of money at a time."

"The grant agreement stipulates you can't have more than five thousand dollars in unspent money without reporting it. You had the finance department prepare reports with false data so you would appear to be in compliance."

"Ridiculous. That's not a crime. The finance department would have told me that we couldn't do that."

"They should have," Irene agreed. "But they didn't. And I think most lawyers could make the case that you would have punished them if they had defied you. We have reports from several departments that if they didn't do what you wanted, you denied them funds, no matter if they were in the budget or not."

Lynda stood up suddenly, as though mounting her soap box. "We're trying to save the taxpayers money. A budget doesn't mean anything. It's cash that's important."

"A budget is a publicly approved plan for spending. Any changes need to go through a public process."

Lynda dismissed that with a wave. "The public doesn't need to know every little thing."

"On the contrary, the public does get to know 'every little thing.' And you know that."

"That's silly."

"Before you became mayor," Irene said smoothly, "you regularly filed public information requests on the budget process as well as the finance records for the city. In fact, you used them in your campaign."

Lynda looked uneasy. "Well, my staff did."

"No, you." Irene flipped open the report to a marked section and displayed the first in a set of papers. "That's your signature."

Lynda sat down again. "I signed a lot of forms."

"That doesn't mean you aren't responsible for what you sign."

Lynda's nostrils flared, but she had enough control not to say what she so obviously longed to say. "Fine. What is your point?"

"My point, mayor, is that I believe this council would have a strong case to recommend the district attorney file ethics charges against you. Peter and I will also take this up with the state prosecutorial team."

"I never embezzled anything." Lynda repeated.

"But you asked employees under your direction to follow irregular accounting principles."

"Surely," Lynda said, obviously trying to sound

calm, "if they did something wrong, that's their problem."

"Oh, they'll have problems," Rusty interrupted, clearly imagining his own future.

"But in this case," Irene said, "I think the buck will stop with you."

"So, if I'm capable of all this, why don't you think I'm the embezzler?" she sneered.

Calmly, Irene took out a second report and laid it next to the first. "Because the embezzling has been going on since before you were mayor."

Chapter 29

Irene had been waiting for one final piece of information. She received the photo after lunch and she worked with the police and DA Gary Boyd for the necessary approvals, then asked the suspect to join her in a conference room.

A few minutes later, Kathy Nicols walked into the room. Seeing Peter, Rusty, and Jayne were in the room as well, she stopped abruptly.

"Thanks for coming," Irene said. "Please have a seat."

Kathy looked worried but sat down at the table.

"I'll get right to it," Irene said. "Over the last three weeks, we have discovered eighteen checks that had been cut to a Willamette Falls Consulting, Inc. We could find no corresponding authorization for the purchases. When we investigated further, we discovered that this company did not exist. Upon getting warrants, we discovered the money was being transferred into a series of accounts that eventually led to the account of a Rachel Moore."

"When we investigated Rachel Moore, we discovered she had died two years ago. We then discovered she had died as a result of complications from a 2005 car crash that put her into a coma.

"During the period between 2005-2015 her medical bills and all expenses were paid with the insurance settlement from the driver of the at-fault vehicle. She also collected disability and social security. This money was deposited into her account and withdrawn via an ATM card in cash.

"When Ms. Moore died in 2015, her accounts did not close. Instead, account activity picked up substantially. Amounts of several thousand were regularly made into the account, transferred, and eventually removed via ATM withdrawals."

Irene pushed a printout of an ATM video still across the table. "My colleague was able to get this video from three weeks ago. This was the last withdrawal from that account."

A surprisingly sharp and clear video frame showed Kathy withdrawing a wad of bills.

"Kathy, you are the daughter of Rachel Moore. When your mother was injured, you were made her legal guardian. Though your mother's care was completely paid for with the insurance settlement, you applied for disability and social security on her behalf and used that cash for yourself."

"It wasn't for me," Kathy said angrily. "It was for her. They said they covered everything, but it wasn't enough to make anything nice."

"That's an interesting point," Irene said. "During those ten years you were living in Arizona while your mother was in a center in Portland."

Kathy looked down at her hands. Irene noticed she had started to twist her wedding ring. "I used it to send her things," she said defensively.

"You are an experienced finance worker. When you started at the City of Lakelynn, you recognized the internal weaknesses of the finance department. You created a vendor named Willamette Falls Consulting and started slipping small requests into accounts payable system. You were able to conceal these small payments by doctoring bank statements, adding the amount to another vendor so everything balanced.

"For the first few years, the amounts were relatively small. Under the amount that would have required a personal signature. You had access to a copy of the city's signature stamp, so no one but you saw the actual checks. Then you got bolder. In the last six months, you have withdrawn more than in the first four years." Irene pushed a spreadsheet of the applicable checks across the table.

Kathy didn't look at the spreadsheet, looking down and twisting her ring.

"Initially, Kathy was able to enter the bills herself. At some point the procedure changed and accounts payable added their initials when they entered payments. She recognized that check stock security was lax and started to use this to her advantage, regularly destroying check series to hide evidence.

"But the most egregious flaw, the one that let you get away with it, was that no one was using the original banking statements to reconcile the accounts. The finance department depended solely on the downloaded records. Kathy started providing them, discouraging anyone else from looking at banking records. She used the city's graphic design software to set up a dummy bank statement."

Irene displayed a photo, provided by Rusty, of Kathy's computer. A folder marked *bank statements* had been opened. Two files were listed for each period, the second labeled with a suffix attributable to a well-known publishing software.

"You aren't the only person with access. I honestly didn't know if it was you or Betty. I suspected it was not Betty because her personality type does not fit the crime. And you were so insistent that having original bank statements was unnecessary, which seemed out of character."

Irene studied Kathy. Her eyes were bright, her face was fierce, but she didn't respond.

"I want a lawyer," Kathy finally spit out.

Irene nodded. Kathy had been a wary adversary, covering her tracks at almost every turn. She was controlled enough to keep silent after she saw the cause was lost. Irene pondered her claim that the extra money had been to make things nice for her mother.

It might have started out that way.

****

Irene and Peter walked with Rusty and Jayne to the nearby, much-frequented coffee shop. After they had placed their orders, the four sat around a table in the corner.

"So, that's the end of it?" Rusty asked.

Irene shook her head. "Probably not. There could be a trial, or even two. But the rest of our work can be done in Salem."

"I'm still not sure I understand everything," Jayne said tiredly. "Lynda didn't take any money, but she was still committing fraud. What are we going to do? The police haven't taken her into custody."

"The City of Lakelynn is going to have to do some hard work," Irene warned. "I'll recommend that the state file ethics charges against her, but unless more evidence comes to light, a criminal conviction is unlikely. A smart lawyer would argue the revenue manipulation was part of a management strategy, and didn't benefit the mayor personally. The city council might consider filing in civil court for damages."

"What about the audit?" Rusty asked.

Peter answered. "Once the audit is finished and the opinion issued, you'll have to draft the management response. You should probably prepare for a federal audit at some point. The auditor will be able to help you correct the accounting and program deficiencies."

Irene's eyes met Rusty's. They exchanged a sad, knowing look.

"You should work with other city managers and get some advice about installing stricter internal controls, revising the budget process, and modifying the reporting system," Irene advised. "The council sets out the to-do list and the city workers do it."

"Betty obviously can't continue as the finance director," Rusty mused. "That's going to be its own set of headaches."

"You might ask Rose," Irene suggested.

"Yeah, she's good," Rusty agreed. "But she doesn't want the job. I asked once."

Irene smiled. "I bet she'll help you out."

A solemn silence fell.

"It's ironic," Irene mused. "We never did discover what happened to the missing check stock that started this whole thing."

Peter snorted.

"I forgot about that," said Rusty.

Another silence.

Miserably, Jayne admitted, "I feel bad for not paying better attention."

"You can't take responsibility for everything," Irene heard herself say. "Other people have duties and responsibilities."

"It's impossible for one person to prevent every problem or solve every oversight. You have to give people a chance to take on more responsibility." Peter smiled at Jayne sympathetically. "Remember, no one is forced to say yes."

Jayne looked up at the ceiling, clearly trying to control tears. "The publicity will be a nightmare," Jayne mused bitterly.

No one responded.

"Peter, are you ready? I'd like to get going." Irene pulled out her purse.

"It was nice to meet you," Jayne said, "even under the circumstances."

Irene smiled. "That's a nice thing to say."

Chapter 30

Once inside her car, Irene dug through her purse to find a pain killer. Her shoulder throbbed and a tension headache squeezed her temples. She dry-swallowed the pills. Home was less than an hour away.

It wasn't only the day at Lakelynn. The argument with Angie ached like a sore tooth. Her own hostility frightened her. She had marched through the last few days with bitter resolution, as if the city interviews were a punishment for the fight.

She realized she wasn't only stressed; she was furious.

At her body.

At her doctors.

At her family.

At her friends.

At having to stop dog agility with Percy.

At having to stop spending unlimited time with her nephews.

And at this case. What kind of world was it? Trying to forestall the sneaky, the devious, the crooks. Make accommodations for the incompetent, the snowflakes, the windbags. To stop a daughter from stealing money from her own mother.

Angry tears welled up, but Irene took a deep breath. She kept driving, kept blinking.

When she pulled up to the house, she heard Percy's

excited panting. He waited at the gate, then would rush around to the back door when she entered. She smiled. Every day, the same routine. No matter how late she was.

And as abruptly as the anger came, it left, leaving only tiredness in its place. She had her dog. She had her life. They'd muddle through.

She went inside, intending for the first time to follow up on some of the suggestions friends and doctors had been throwing at her.

****

Ignoring her boss's hint that work was backing up, Irene took the next day off. She started her day at the normal time with the usual tasks but lingered over coffee. Sharon knocked on the back door.

"Come in," Irene called.

Sharon let herself and Mule in the house. As Mule was as familiar with this house as his own, he padded around to see if there was any leftover food. When he had circled the room, he came to Irene and leaned against her sorrowfully. Percy chaperoned them from his cushion under the counter. Irene took the top off the cookie jar and passed one little bone to each dog. The dogs went to separate corners to scarf down the treats, then inspected the other's corner for crumbs.

Sharon laughed. "They never figure out the other one didn't miss anything."

Irene smiled. "How are you?'"

Sharon rolled her eyes. "Some days I wonder what possessed me to try to build a center full of people like me. We're all on our own planet. No one can get anything done."

Irene laughed, as Sharon had intended her to.

"You're still here?" Sharon commented.

"You should be proud of me. I'm taking the day off."

"Break out the band. Mark the day on the calendar. Go buy a lottery ticket," Sharon crowed. "Irene Lisner is taking a day off."

"Indeed." Irene took a sip coffee. The two fell into companionable silence. "What's your plan for the day?"

Sharon shrugged. "Ride herd on the center. Irritate Carrie. Walk the dog. How about you?" Carrie was Sharon's life partner who worked at a local non-profit women's shelter.

Irene shrugged. "I need to make up with Angie."

Sharon nodded.

"I've been sitting here trying to figure out how," Irene confessed. "I'm so tired."

"Maybe you shouldn't be focusing on solutions," Sharon said gently. "Be honest. Tell her what's going on. You can't do everything. It's her job to figure out the solution of how to cope with that."

"If I tell her, Jennifer will find out."

"Yes. And that's not the end of the world. She is your mother."

Irene rolled her eyes.

"I think you don't want to tell her because then you'd have to admit that you can't do everything yourself."

Irene glared at Sharon.

"The truth hurts, doesn't it?" Sharon teased.

"I'm not going to give you any more coffee," Irene grumbled.

Sharon chuckled. She leaned across the table and tapped the newspaper next to Irene. "Big story this morning." She waited meaningfully.

Irene nodded.

"I caught the mayor's press conference last night."

Irene groaned. "What did she say?"

"She announced that she was going to resign and went on a tirade about how the OA—" Sharon winked. "—was out to get her and how it was unfair that we lived in a society where there was no longer freedom for cities to clean up their own problems. She said that she saw that it was useless to try to 'solve anything' at a local level and she was going to devote her time a bigger cause."

"Did the newscast show the whole speech?"

"No. Just a few soundbites. Then one of the council members read a statement that said the council was in full support of the mayor's decision."

Irene shook her head. "When I left last night, I got the impression she was going to tough it out."

"Well, something changed her mind."

"I talked to the ethics office," Irene admitted. "They had been on the verge of filing ethics charges against the mayor before this investigation." She sighed. "One thing we didn't catch was the Red Wren contract. Apparently, they were giving her free PR consulting as long as the city kept throwing extra work their way. She'd rammed through a couple of amendments to their existing contact but never revealed that she was getting a kickback."

Sharon whistled.

"And Peter texted me that the local paper is planning a special issue, going over every detail."

"No one should get good press from this," Sharon pointed out.

"True," Irene agreed, "but I hate to see a trial by public opinion. It feels like a hollow victory."

****

After Sharon left, Irene texted Angie.

—*You working today?*—

Irene finished cleaning her kitchen before the reply came back.

—*This afternoon.*—

Irene huffed.

—*Can I come and see you this morning? We need to talk.*—

A long pause.

—*Yes.*—

Figuring this was as much as Angie would concede, Irene set up Percy in the backyard with fresh water and a frozen treat, then grabbed her purse and hit the road. The mid-morning traffic moved briskly, and thirty minutes later she pulled up in front of Angie's townhouse. As she knocked on the door, she heard the unmistakable sound of the scuffle.

"You've had two turns. It's my turn."

"No, I didn't."

Sounds of grunting.

Crash.

Before Irene had time to decide whether to simply enter and make sure everything was okay or continue waiting, the door was flung open. Angie moved back down the hall so quickly that Irene only saw the end of her skirt as she rounded the corner in the other direction.

"I don't care who started it," she barked. "Both of you stop it."

Irene found the boys ensconced on separate sofas, arms angrily folded across their chests. Dave's face was the picture of stubborn determination, but Mike's face showed signs of recent tears. A large jumble of blocks, trains, and building blocks was scattered across the floor. Irene surmised the toys were the cause of the crash.

"Time out for both of you," Angie growled. The boys groaned. "Go up to your rooms and ponder the error of your ways. I'll call you when you can come down." She snatched the e-pads from the coffee table. "No e-pads while you're there."

Dave furiously stomped up to his room, ignoring both adults, but Mike ran over to Irene, clearly expecting her to somehow overturn the ruling. He gave her a hug. She patted his shoulder and gently nudged him away. "You heard her." With exaggerated stomps, Mike headed up the stairs, too.

Angie and Irene were left facing each other. With a sigh, Angie picked up her phone and set a timer. "Do you want a cup of coffee?"

Irene smiled, recognizing it as a truce signal. "I rarely turn one down."

A few minutes later, they seated at the kitchen table. Angie spun her coffee mug. Irene fiddled with the spoon she had used to stir her coffee. Both of them jumped when Angie's phone buzzed.

"That's the boys' time-out." She picked up the e-pads and put them on a charger set up within a nearby bookshelf. "I'll go tell them they can come down."

Irene took a deep breath. "I need to talk to you. Without them. Is there a chance they'll stay in their rooms?

Angie studied her, then decided. "They've been on the rampage all morning. They need quiet time. Apart." When she came down, Irene could hear music playing softly. "Mike was asleep on his bean bag. He'll be out for thirty minutes. I let Dave listen to music and get out his marble racers for quiet play."

"Thanks." Irene took a sip of coffee. "It's been a long time since Mike took a nap."

"He drops out every once in a while, usually after he and Dave go a few rounds." Angie sighed. "It's been more than a few rounds today."

"Jason is working?"

"He took the morning shift. The sitter comes at one, and then I'll head out. Fridays are busy at both dealerships."

Irene nodded.

Once again, they dropped into awkward silence.

Irene broke it. "I'm sorry, Angie. I'm sorry I lashed out at you for asking about my health. And I'm sorry for what I said about you not caring about me except for when you needed me."

Angie studied her. "I'm sorry, too. I think I do lean on you too much. You're so steady and dependable. You always have been."

Irene felt a tear, and quickly dropped her head to study her coffee, hoping to hide it. "I don't want to stop being steady and dependable for you and the boys." She took a deep breath. "But I am going to have to make some lifestyle changes that will affect my relationship with all of you." She took another deep breath. "I've been diagnosed with MS. Multiple Sclerosis."

Angie stared at her.

With difficulty, Irene continued. "I've been working with the doctor for about six months. I got the final results a couple weeks ago. Relapsing Remitting Multiple Sclerosis."

"I've never heard of that," Angie said. "Is there more than one type?"

"Yes. This type is considered the less severe. I might be able to go through long periods without any problems. But right now, I'm having problems."

Angie looked shaken. Finally, in a quiet voice, she asked, "Are you okay? I mean, emotionally?"

Irene met her eyes. She thought about brushing her sister off. "No. I'm not."

Angie nodded. "Do you want to talk about it?"

"God, no."

She smiled. "I felt like it was a safe question."

Silence. Angie leaned across the table to take Irene's hand. The touch was comforting.

"Have you told Jennifer?

Irene shook her head. "I will. But not now."

They stayed like that for a few more moments.

"Why don't you call off the sitter and I'll take the boys overnight," Irene volunteered. "We could hike Silver Falls State Park, go to a baseball game, and I can drop them off tomorrow morning."

"Are you sure you're up to that?" Angie said in surprise.

"I love spending time with them." Irene paused. "But I need to be careful about trying to do too much. You know that's hard for me, but my feet are being held to the fire. Like the universe is saying 'You must find balance.' "

Angie smiled wanly. "Join the club." The silence dragged out between them. "Jason and I had a big fight last night. He left to stay in a motel."

Irene didn't say anything but kept a sympathetic look on her face.

Angie continued. "I know he's frustrated. Having two kids and working isn't exciting. But both of us knew what we were getting into. The boys deserve security," she said fiercely, as though repeating something from the argument. "I don't want to move to Colorado," she muttered.

"Is that what he wants to do?"

Angie grunted. "Who knows what Jason wants? It's his latest idea. He's got a buddy he says can get us set up, helping him with guiding rock climbers."

Irene struggled for something to say. "Do you want to talk about it?"

Angie smiled. "God, no."

Irene grinned back. "I figured it was a safe question."

Chapter 31

That evening, Mike and Dave cheered the home team from the outfield bleachers. Irene could tell Mike was trying to keep up with Dave, but at the next lull, he snuggled against Irene. "This is different than home," Mike murmured sleepily.

"Uh-huh." Irene stroked his forehead. "It's not on TV."

"No. It's nice to be here."

Irene smiled. "Yes."

"Mom and Dad had a fight last night."

Irene nodded. "Your mom told me. Married people have fights sometimes. It doesn't mean much."

"Dad left."

"He's at work."

"After they fought."

"Don't worry. He'll be back."

"Unnnn." He fell asleep.

For a few minutes, Irene enjoyed his weight on her side. It wouldn't be long before this kind of thing would be only a memory. Dave had mostly moved beyond hugs and cuddling.

Her arm tingled. She shifted, and Mike curled up in his own chair. Her arm kept tingling in a way that was becoming familiar. Her heart clutched; she wouldn't be able to drive them home. She reached for her phone, struggling to get her hands to cooperate.

"Dave, can you get my cell phone?" she asked, and shifted her hip to give him access.

He continued watching the outfield with rapt attention. "Dave." He looked at her. "I need you get my phone."

He made a face. "They are about to change batters."

"Dave. Do it now."

He reached into her pocket and pulled it out, holding it out irritably.

"Thank you. Can you call Sharon and put it on speaker phone?"

Looking interested, he whipped his way through the menus and held it up.

"Hi." Sharon chirped.

"Hey, Sharon."

"How's it going?"

Irene said her next words carefully. "Actually, my nephews and I are at Keizer Stadium at a baseball game, and we need a ride home."

"A ride home? How did you get there?"

"I drove. But we need a ride home."

There was silence, then Sharon said, "I'll call you when I get there."

"Thanks."

A half-hour later, after being dropped off at the stadium by a taxi, Sharon called. Dave carried the backpack with their items, Mike carried the souvenirs, and they used the elevator to exit the stadium.

Sharon waited at the entrance. "Hey. How was the game?"

Both boys were well acquainted with Sharon and didn't hesitate to regale her with the amazing details. Irene quietly passed Sharon the car keys before sitting down on the bench. Sharon examined her, then gathered up the boys. "Let's get the car and bring it back to pick up Irene. Can you tell me where you parked?"

Excited to be in charge of anything, the boys raced to show her where the car was.

Once home, Sharon helped get the boys in the house and to bed.

Irene sat in the kitchen, her hands trembling.

"You got up, took the dog for a walk, hiked with your nephews, and then went to a baseball game." Calmly, Sharon made cups of tea. "Look at your Fitbit."

Irene got the watch to light up. "17,533 steps. I was tired, but I never thought about it." Percy came over and laid his head in her lap. She fondled his ears absently.

"Nothing major happened," Sharon soothed. "Make a note. That's too much. You'll have to recalibrate what you can do now."

"Right now, it feels like I can't do anything."

Sharon gave her a steady look. "You're still sorting out what you can and can't do. If I was in your shoes, it would have never occurred to me that this might be different. So, now you've learned something."

Irene rubbed her neck. "The doctor said exercise was good."

"I'm sure it is. But over-exertion isn't. Have you thought about the class I was talking about?"

"Yes," Irene admitted. "I don't want you to start something just for me."

"It's not just for you. There are other clients." Sharon paused. "Have you thought about going to see a therapist? This is a big change."

Irene was unable to help the note of petulance in her voice. "I've thought about it."

Sharon heard it, too, and changed the subject. "Why are the boys here for the weekend? I thought you were going to take it easy?"

Irene explained her day off and visit to Angie. "I love spending time with them, especially if we have a plan."

Sharon's nostrils flared. "So, instead of taking it easy, you decided to run after two boys for the weekend. Way to follow doctor's orders."

"Stop talking to me like that," Irene growled. "I'm an adult and I get to choose what I do."

"Are you?" Sharon shot back. "An adult? Could have fooled me."

Irene glared at her.

Sharon shook her head. "Sorry. Knee-jerk reaction to Angie taking advantage."

"This was my idea. Not hers."

Sharon grunted.

Irene had stopped trembling. She got up from the table to get her purse. "How much do I owe you for the cab?"

"Don't insult me."

Irene held out a bill. "Don't insult me by not accepting my thanks."

Sharon frowned at her as she took the money. "All right." She gave Irene a hug. "I'll stop by tomorrow if I can." Percy got his ears scratched on her way out.

****

Saturday morning, Irene and the boys went out for pancakes, then had a video game marathon. Angie was due to came by to pick up the boys about noon. In spite of the huge stack of pancakes they had consumed, but by midmorning they were exhibiting signs of hunger. Irene set out snacks, then took out a pack of cards to begin a game of knock poker.

"I'll take two," Dave announced.

"Knock," Mike crowed, and they all laughed.

Percy ran to the door, announcing someone was there.

Mike jumped up to open the door. "Jenny," he crowed happily.

Jennifer stood at the door, looking both gorgeous and confused. She bent down to give Mike a hug, then looked quizzically around the room. "I didn't realize you had the boys."

Dave and Mike regaled her with the details of yesterday's hike, the baseball game, and the pancakes.

"Don't you guys look happy!" Jennifer commented.

"I'm expecting Angie in a few minutes to collect them," Irene explained, then saw Angie's car pull into the driveway.

"Mom." The boys abandoned Jennifer as if they hadn't seen their mother in weeks.

Ten minutes later, Irene, Angie, and Jennifer were at the table, playing another round of cards. The boys chose to finish out their video game.

Irene took a deep breath. "I'd like to tell you both what's been going on."

Jennifer looked up from studying her cards. "Something's going on?"

Irene nodded. "I've had some medical issues the last few months."

"That silly dog stuff," Jennifer said, going back to adjusting her cards.

Angie remained quiet.

"A couple of weeks ago, I was diagnosed with

Multiple Sclerosis. I told Angie yesterday, and I thought it would be a good idea to let you know, too."

Jennifer turned to view me with wide eyes. "MS? A woman at church has that. Aren't there different kinds?"

"It's possible someone at church has it. And yes, there are different types. The doctors tell me mine is the kind that progresses slowly, with periods of normalcy."

"Periods of normalcy?" Jennifer repeated.

Irene nodded, studying her cards as though her life depended on them. "Currently, I'm having attacks—"

"Right now?" Jennifer looked alarmed. "Should we take you to the emergency room?"

"No. I've been having new symptoms over the last few weeks. But they tell me that with medication and lifestyle changes, I could have months or even years of no symptoms."

"So," Angie began, "after you told me the other day, I looked up MS. It's your immune system attacking the protective covering of your nerves. The big concern is that the nerves can deteriorate and become permanently damaged." She studied Irene. "Is that what the doctors think will happen?"

Irene shook her head but also shrugged. "It's possible. They hope with the newer medications and some lifestyle adjustments, I'll have a good chance of getting it under control."

"Is it hereditary?" Jennifer asked.

"No one knows what causes it. They tell me a combination of genetics and environmental factors appears to be responsible. Apparently, the Willamette Valley has one of the highest instances of MS in the world."

Both Angie and Jennifer looked startled.

"Should we be worried?" Jennifer asked.

"It's not catching. But if any of your limbs start to go numb or you have numbness, you should probably talk to your doctor."

"What kind of lifestyle changes do the doctors want you to make?" Angie asked suspiciously.

Irene smiled at her sheepishly. "I need to live my life but be careful about what I do. I need to cut back on stress. I'm going to start a specialized yoga class that may help with symptoms or regaining balance I've lost." Irene took a deep breath. "I'm going to stop doing agility for a while. The running is too hard on me and my timing isn't good enough, at least right now."

"Wow," Angie murmured. "That's hard. Are you okay?"

Irene shook her head, feeling her eyes moisten. She looked up to study the ceiling.

"I'm sorry," Jennifer said. She reached across the table to take my hand. "I know how you loved it."

Irene was surprised. She met her mother's gaze, then squeezed back.

"So," Angie said. "What can we do to help?"

Irene smiled wryly. "Unfortunately, I don't think there is much you can do, but I'm not going to be able to help as much with the boys. I never know when I might have an attack." She described the events of the evening before. "I can't drive the kids around, which means babysitting is going to be limited."

"Should you be driving at all?" Jennifer asked.

"Right now, the doctor says it's okay. I'm learning to watch for the warning signs. If I get stuck somewhere, I'll have to think about what I'm going to do. I've talked to my boss about the possibility of limiting travel."

"If you have any trouble, I know an excellent attorney," Jennifer announced.

"I don't think I need a lawyer right now, but it's good to know I have options."

Jennifer looked skeptical.

"In the meantime," Irene pushed away from the table, "I'm going to be working to make some changes at work and to my lifestyle. I wanted you guys to know what was going on. I may not be able to do some things, especially spur-of-the-moment."

Jennifer took offense. "What does that mean? Are you accusing us of something?"

"I'm not accusing anyone of anything. But"—she put an emphasis on the word and gave Jennifer a direct look—"if I say I can't do something, it means I can't do it." She turned to Angie. "That goes for babysitting." Then she turned back to Jennifer. "Or helping you with showings. Or making coffee at church. Or extra accounting."

She sniffed. "You never do those things anyway."

"Yet you're always asking me to do them." Irene reached her hand across the table to cover Jennifer's hand. "I need you to respect my space."

"You always want space," Jennifer said tartly.

"Maybe I always need space." Irene reached over to cover Angie's hand, too. "We're very different people, but I love you both."

Angie reached out and covered Jennifer's other hand. She squeezed. "You're stubborn, but that doesn't mean we don't love you."

Irene squeezed their hands back. "It's the family trait."

Mike and Dave ran back into the kitchen. "We got a

high score."

"Get your things, crew," Angie said, releasing her sister and mother. "We're meeting your dad at the monster truck rally."

"Yeah!" They scrambled to get their bags.

"I better get moving, too," Jennifer said. "I had a few minutes between appointments and thought I'd stop by."

Irene nodded. "I'm glad you came."

Jennifer sniffed. "I wish you'd told me the boys were here. I would have brought them something."

Angie laughed. "I think they'll cope."

Irene smiled and gave them both a hug. They weren't perfect, but neither was she.

Epilogue

City of Lakelynn Releases Forensic Audit

A forensic audit commissioned by the City of Lakelynn following the city's discovery of fraudulent activities by the former finance director was released today by Renee Downy, the new city manager.

"This report essentially confirmed the criminal investigation carried out by the police and the OA in terms of the magnitude of the loss. It sheds additional light on how it was accomplished," Downy said.

In a letter accompanying the report to Downy, the auditors stated, "Based on the results of our fraud investigations, we find that there is sufficient evidence to support the conclusion that $132,779.21 was misappropriated from the City of Lakelynn by former city employee, Kathy Nicols.

The loss cited in the auditor's letter is less than the originally suspected amount quoted by investigators. The six-figure fraud took place over a five-year period beginning in 2012.

Kathy Nicols' employment with Lakelynn ended earlier this year with her arrest. Nicols pleaded guilty to 57 counts of felony theft. She is awaiting sentencing at Clackamas County Circuit Court next month.

Since this arrest, the already beleaguered city has lost a number of its employees. The city council decided not to renew then-City Manager Russell Barrett's contract.

Lakelynn hired a private accounting firm in August to get the city in compliance. When the fraud was uncovered, the Oregon Office of Adjudication was consulted. Employees at the Office of Adjudication were able to uncover and identify the embezzlement.

Upon turning in their final audit opinion in September, the private accounting firm noted discrepancies in checking statements and copies of checks received by the city from the bank, but found it, "difficult to distinguish between error and intent to conceal due to the poor state of accounting oversight."

The auditors found multiple, uncorrected bookkeeping errors relating to the banking activities, under-reporting of cash receipts, and undocumented adjustments to year-end balances, among other problems.

The most senior private auditor wrote: "General ledger account reconciliations were often performed well after the month and/or fiscal year had ended. Given the myriad of uncorrected errors and journal entries made within the general ledger, it would be inordinately cost-prohibitive to ascertain to what extend individual funds or departments may have been affected by the alleged embezzlement."

A word about the author…

Tara Choate writes from her home base of Lincoln City, Oregon. A native Oregonian, she has had a varied career around the state. Tara is supervised by her rescue dog, Key, and two cats, Chitza and Anouk. Since getting her first dog, she has enjoyed competing with her dogs in dog agility, but shifted her focus to canine nose work as age caught up with her. Tara is also a watercolor artist. You can view a gallery of Tara's works, upcoming events, works in progress, and upcoming titles at www.tarachoate.com.